THE
BRAVEST
WORD

THE BRAVEST WORD

KATE FOSTER

WALKER
BOOKS

For Dad

First published in Great Britain 2024 by Walker Books Ltd
87 Vauxhall Walk, London SE11 5HJ

2 4 6 8 10 9 7 5 3 1

Text © 2022 Kate Foster
Cover illustration © 2024 Thy Bui

This book has been typeset in ITC Garamond Pro

Printed and bound by CPI Group (UK) Ltd, Croydon CR0 4YY

British Library Cataloguing in Publication Data:
a catalogue record for this book is
available from the British Library

ISBN 978-1-5295-1421-6

www.walker.co.uk

MIX
Paper | Supporting
responsible forestry
FSC® C171272

1

I can't do this.

I can't do this.

But it's happening.

I *am* doing this.

I'm following my teammates onto the pitch. I'm watching my orange boots, brand new for the brand new season, take step after step across the short grass. I wish I could stop, spin around and run home.

I can't pick out their voices from all the shouting and cheering and referees' whistles in the other matches surrounding the central pitch – the pitch I play on, reserved for the best teams – but I know my parents are yelling encouragement from their usual spot on the clubhouse verandah with all the other parents. And Mum's voice will be the loudest of all.

Even though this is only a friendly pre-season game, how can I possibly let her down – again?

I stumble forward as Joseph shoves me in the shoulder.

"We've got to smash this team today, Matt," he says.

I fake a laugh. "Definitely," I reply.

His toothy grin drops and his expression turns into a snarl. Joseph's a pretty good midfielder, but we're not friends or anything. I've known him since primary school. But, since we started high school last month, he's been hanging around with loads more girls and a horrible bunch who pick on everyone. As for his PicRoll account, it's mainly people swearing and arguing and talking trash to anyone who doesn't agree with their opinions. He's got his reasons, but still, it's not a nice way to use social media.

"Look at that massive kid." He points. "There's no way he's an under twelve."

My eyes follow his muddy finger even though I do *not* want to look because I've already seen the boy he's talking about. But, like I always do, I swallow down what I'd prefer to do, what I *want* to do, and check out our opposition warming up and the tall striker who looks like he visits the gym every day. We've played this team before, but I don't remember him from last season. He's either new or has doubled in size. His white-and-blue-striped jersey with the black number nine on the back rides up as he lurches to head the ball away.

Truth is, I know I'm a better football player than

him, but it's like my brain doesn't care about any of that right now, like it doesn't believe it. As a defender it's my job to hassle the strikers, mark them tight so I take them out of the game. I know for a fact I'll end up marking him. I always go up against the toughest or fastest players, because Stu, my coach, is convinced I can handle anything.

I used to be able to.

Not any more.

But I can't tell anyone this. It's embarrassing. Me: player of the year for the past two years – my mum's pride and joy.

Nope. No way. Never.

I tried mentioning something to Dad a few weeks ago, but Mum butted in on the conversation, telling me I'm the best and no one will ever get past me. To stop being so silly. My mum is all about getting on with things; it's her way.

And I *am* being silly … but there are other things, too. Other things I've noticed over the last couple of months.

The way my chest tightens all the time and my stomach dive-bombs; the way I'm always forgetting what I'm in the middle of doing; the way I don't like any of the things I used to – football, gaming, hanging out with my mates. And how tired I feel all the time.

So tired. I wish I knew why. I can't figure out what's changed.

"Right, sit down, boys."

I startle at Stu's voice, my heart pounding a fast rhythm, faster even than before, as I realize my team have reached our bench.

"Settle down. Sit."

I need to listen; I have to keep away from my thoughts. I perch on the edge of the wooden slats in the corner of our shelter, focusing on my clenched fists that rest on my knees and pressing my soles into the floor through my tight boots.

"Right, big game today. Last friendly before the season kicks off. We need our heads out of the clouds. No more than two touches each…"

Stu rambles on with the same team talk we have before every match, one I'm so familiar with I could recite it myself, but my concentration is moving away no matter how much I try to take in his words. The harder I try to listen, the more my brain rebels. And I'm thinking about everything and nothing all at the same time.

But mostly I'm thinking about ways to get out of playing this match.

The logical part of my brain tells me to toughen up, as Mum would say.

I can't do this.

I can't do this.

"Matt, you listening?"

I nod, concentrating on Stu's face. He frowns at me and rubs a hand over his bald head before putting on his red Whaleview Soccer Club cap. "OK, we need world-class Matt on the pitch today, got it? Not the Matt we've had in the last matches."

My cheeks burn red hot, and I don't miss the chuckles from some of my teammates, including a weird huff-growl from Joseph. I glance over at Ted, my best mate, and he gives me a nod and a thumbs-up. I look away, not really sure if I smiled at him even though I meant to, and nod to Stu again.

"Got it, coach," I reply, mustering whatever confidence I can into my voice.

"Straighten out that head of yours and let's win this."

I nod again, wishing and begging the attention to move away from me. He eyeballs me for a moment longer with those sharp light-blue eyes and then claps once, loud and firm, startling me again. My breath catches but I turn it into a throat clear, and then clap and chant with the rest of the Whales Under 12s A Squad – the unstoppable three-time champions, three years in a row.

And now it's too late.

I'm going out on the pitch and playing this game whether I like it or not. This moment used to be my favourite. The buzz, the adrenaline, the apprehension. I don't get why I don't feel this way now. What's changed since last year?

I've failed to find a way out and desperation has lodged in my chest. I jog over to our goal to get in position for the referee's whistle, legs feeling like they're going to give way at any second. Ted pats my shoulder as he runs past into his left-back position.

"You OK?" he asks, jogging backwards, his black curls bouncing up and down.

"Yeah, cool mate," I reply. But it's there, the shake in my voice, the empty feeling in my chest, the screaming in my head, in my ears, and the numbness of my limbs. I'm so not cool.

Stu's right: I need to straighten my head out.

Ted nods, and I watch his red shirt with the number sixteen on the back move away.

I can't do this.

The whistle screeches and I move forward with the back line, pushing up and out of our goal mouth, light on my toes but heavy in my gut. My breaths are an effort and pressured, panic charging through me like I've never felt before, almost burning my skin. It's like my chest is going to explode and my insides will splatter on the field. Once again Mum and Dad pop into my mind, and I swear this time I *can* hear Mum shrieking my name.

I can't do this.

I need to get off this pitch, now.

Their midfield has the ball. They're passing quick: one touch then pass, moving all the time, keeping my teammates working hard, calling instructions, warning each other.

I vaguely register Stu bellowing my name and I know where he wants me without having to hear his actual command. So, I draw up all I have from the pit of my belly and charge towards the number nine striker. The kid shoves his arm across me, his elbows high and hard and digging into my chest and shoulder as he tries to muscle me out the way. He calls for the ball, but it sounds weird in my ears. I screw up my face and wince. Everything's muffled and low, like I'm underwater. My heart's going so fast I can't even feel it and I honestly don't think I'm breathing.

The next thing I know I'm on the ground. Flat on my back, staring up at the crystal-blue sky, not a cloud in sight. And I'm hot, so hot. I hear a whistle, voices, words, my name, but I close my eyes and flop onto my side, my head spinning.

"You all right, son?"

I open my eyes and stare into the gaze of an old grey-haired man – the referee. He's got his hand on my arm; I can see it but can't feel it for some reason.

"Did you get an elbow to the head?" he asks.

I think I reply. I mean, I can feel my mouth move, but I have no idea what I say.

"Matt, what's happened?" It's Ted, and then he and the referee help me to my feet, and again I think I'm talking but it's like my voice isn't mine.

Back on my feet I walk, but it feels more like floating, like I'm not actually here and having some kind of out-of-body experience.

I don't remember how, but now I'm sitting on the team bench, head between my knees and I feel so sick. In fact, I know I'm going to spew, even though there's nothing in my belly. I couldn't eat the bacon-and-egg roll Mum made me earlier, like she always does before a game. She told me it was probably nerves. My mouth waters. I struggle up and onto my feet, wobbling, bashing and scraping my arm against the wall of the plastic shelter, leaving behind the voice of Stu and the noise of the match carrying on without me.

I stumble, my chest doing that tight thing again and I want it to stop. I go through the gap in the fence bordering the pitch and then trip, liquid hurling out of my mouth. I fall, onto my front, and I'm still dizzy so I shut my eyes.

I don't know how long I lie here. "Hey, Matthew, it's OK. I'm here."

I smile, maybe only on the inside, but I feel relief at the sound of Dad's deep, gentle voice. I don't hear Mum, but I'm pleased about that right now. She's probably disappointed seeing me leave the pitch before I've even touched the ball. The other friendlies we've played I pretended to feel ill or feigned an injury halfway through. I must be such a let-down.

Now that the sick feeling is subsiding, I'm overcome with shame and hideous, horrible embarrassment.

But I know, deep down, as I listen to Dad telling me it's OK and that it doesn't matter, as he helps me across the football fields to the car, that if I hadn't been sick, if whatever happened to me hadn't happened, I'd have done something else to get out of playing today.

I said I couldn't do it.

And I don't think I'll ever be able to again.

2

I sit on the grass in my neighbour Jane's front yard, dragging a stick side to side as Fifi chases and pounces on it. I smile. Fifi's a Maltese shih-tzu cross and the cutest little dog ever. She yaps a fair amount, all high-pitched and excitable, which annoys Mum but I don't mind it. When you have a face like Fifi's I reckon you've got clearance to bark as much as you want.

She snuffles and play-growls as I circle the stick round my back, swapping hands behind me, and then she tries to leap over my outstretched legs but lands on them and splats on her side. I laugh, even though her claws dig in and scratch my thigh, leaving red lines on my skin as she scrabbles back onto her paws and charges for the stick again.

I could sit out here in the coolness of the shade and play with Fifi all day. I feel so much better than I did earlier and I'm trying my best to ignore the shame slicing through my insides. The minute I got in Dad's truck at football and lay on the back seat, the weird dizziness and nausea faded, and when we pulled up onto the drive of our white three-storey townhouse in the middle of Sarasota Avenue, I had to fight not to cry in relief. I would never admit that though, not the times I feel like crying – let alone the times I do cry – not even to Dad.

Mum's already inside the house. She did ask me a few times if I was OK during the ten-minute journey home, telling me she loves me and that she just wants me to enjoy football like I used to – which pretty much means she's annoyed with me.

Dad has been caught by Jane to talk about something garden-related. Our house is attached to Jane's and there's no fence between the front yards. She's super chatty and kind and has become like a part of the family almost, or as much as Mum's allowed her to. She's always outside pottering, front and back. Even though we rent our house, Dad's responsible for keeping the garden neat and tidy; though I think a lot of the time he comes out here for the peace and quiet of our gated housing complex. I see him tracking clouds ambling through the sky and sipping his tea more than digging and raking and mowing. He and Jane both have a gentle nature.

So I decided that rather than follow Mum and face the "heart-to-heart" – which means lecture – I'd sit outside and play with Fifi for a bit.

I'd love a dog of my own one day, but Mum says I'm too young to understand the responsibility. I'm nearly twelve, not two. And at high school now. I know for a fact I would spend every second I could with my own dog, and I would never expect my parents to look after it. I wish she'd give me a chance. When Mum was twelve she was basically the main carer for all her brothers and sisters because her parents weren't home much, and she's forever telling me that she wants me to stay a carefree child for as long as I can. She had to grow up fast, but it seems she doesn't want me to grow up at all.

I let Fifi have the stick and she plonks down with a grunt, lying parallel with my bare leg, her soft fur brushing against my skin. She gnaws on the stick with the side of her mouth. She's so cute, and I run my hand up and down over her back and head, smiling as her tail swishes.

"Hey, Matty, how was the game?"

"OK, thanks," I reply, my tummy swirling at the lie. I don't want Jane to know what actually happened. I glance at Dad standing beside her, his expression plain and unreadable, but I know he's studying me through his sunglasses.

I look at Jane, both her hands shoved in the front pocket of her apron, the green one we bought her for

Christmas that says *How well is my garden growing? Only thyme will tell.* It's the worst joke ever but Jane loves it. Jane is positive about most things – amazing really, since her husband died a few years back, her daughter lives in Western Australia, and she has all these health problems too. One of the first things she told us as we were literally moving in was how pleased she was to have someone new to talk gardening with. And Jane's been great, even looking after me when I was in primary school on the days Mum and Dad worked late. Now I'm in high school, not so much. I can be home alone. I can be grown up.

"Did you win?" she asks, a small breeze playing with some loose strands of her grey hair.

"Er, yeah, I think so," I answer. Duh, brain. I need to learn to lie better. I stroke Fifi a bit faster and bite the inside of my cheek.

"We had to leave before the end. Matty wasn't feeling too good." Dad to the rescue.

"Ah, that's a shame. I know how much you live for football." She pumps a fist in the air as she says it, her Scottish accent edging through her Australian one when she says "football". She's told me heaps of times how her father and grandfather were the biggest Celtic supporters in the whole of Scotland, so she had no choice but to love football too.

I nod and smile at Jane. And truthfully, I do love football; I've played since I was four years old and am usually heading out on my bike to meet up with Ted and Kai for a kickabout at the park when I'm not training, or they come over and we head out onto the field backing onto my garden.

Usually, but not lately.

"You do look a little pale, my boy," Jane adds, tilting her head to one side. "Maybe a wee sleep this arvo will help."

"Yeah, probably," I answer, nodding.

"Come on then, Matt, let's get inside." Dad says his goodbyes to Jane and heads in through the black front door, indicating for me to follow. I pat Fifi on the head and give her a kiss on her cold, wet nose, then stand and sigh. Hopefully I can at least have a shower to clear my head before Mum has her "talk" with me.

"You haven't played a single full match this year yet. Why, Matthew?"

I roll my head back onto the leather sofa, my neck aching and stiff. I've already told Mum I don't know.

"It's not right to keep letting your team down like this. Honestly, I don't get what's going through your head these days. Football is your love." Her voice is

18

gentle, but every sentence is a question, as if she's exasperated.

I've mentioned to her that I don't get what's going on either; she's pushing for answers I don't have.

"You're their star player, Matty. You won't get that trophy again this year."

I know that. But anyway, I don't deserve the trophy. I don't really deserve to have a place on the team any more.

There's no point me saying anything out loud because Mum isn't listening to me, and I'm scared if I do open my mouth to speak what comes out will be babyish and embarrassing. To be honest, I'm too tired to speak anyway.

I sink lower into the squashy chair, flicking my thumbnails together and chewing the inside of my cheek. I glance over at Dad, who sits next to Mum on the brown leather two-seater. She's prattling on about how much I need to enjoy being young while I can, alternating with *"Do you know how much football fees are?"* and how I should and can talk to her if there's a problem.

Yeah, right.

I love my mum; she's super kind, is my biggest cheerleader and tells the funniest stories about her customers at the hair salon – but she doesn't know how

19

to listen, not just to me but to anyone. She's forever talking over people and finishing their sentences. It's so cringe. But we always let Mum get away with it. It's all part of who she is.

She had a difficult childhood – she tells us of how she didn't finish high school because she had to get a job at fifteen to buy food for her siblings. I can't imagine how hard it must have been and it's definitely made her tough. Though I think too tough sometimes. Apart from Jane occasionally, we've never been close to any other family, except Grandad Cliff when he was alive, Dad's dad, and that's just the way Mum likes it.

But, maybe she's right. Maybe I'd never have coped if I'd been in her shoes.

Dad shoots me a closed-lip smile, his hands folded across his belly.

I rub my eyes, tiredness draping like the heaviest blanket over my body. I smell the lavender soap from my shower and drag in a deep, deep breath until my head buzzes and lightens.

Whether I like it or not, the tears are about to fall. I'm so pathetic.

I feel the wet on my fingertips and my next breath shudders as I exhale and then inhale.

I'm breaking, but I fight the tears away. No way I'm crying over this.

"I'm sorry." The words come out so quiet, and without removing my fingers from my eyes, I get a hold of myself and say it again, louder. "I'm sorry."

The cushion beside me dips, and Mum's perfume envelops me along with her arms. "Matthew, I love you so much, honey. You know that."

I do know that. She tells me a million times a day.

"I don't want you to apologize, just get back to the old Matty."

I let her draw me closer and nod into her shoulder, my tears subsiding as I focus on the softness of her top instead of my stupid behaviour. She squeezes me tight.

"It's OK. It'll all be OK," she says.

But I don't think it will. And her words suddenly irritate me. I don't understand any of it: me, life, anything. And in a flash, that irritation turns into a ball of anger rushing to the surface. I push away from Mum and drive my fists into my eyes harder, holding in all the words I want to yell at her. Ugh, what kind of kid yells at their mum for giving them a hug?

Dad must be crouching in front of me now, as I feel his big, firm hands on my bare knees.

Knowing he's there calms me and I breathe a little deeper. After a few minutes, or seconds maybe, I scrub at my face, rubbing away all the dregs of sadness and anger, and look at Dad through blurry tears.

He pats my knee. "It's just football. A silly old game where people try to kick some sphere past a rectangular frame."

I force a smile to show I appreciate his joke.

I collapse back on the sofa, a sudden need to be alone, feeling cold and hot all at once. I lay my head on my Wolves cushion. Wolves was Grandad Cliff's favourite football team, and after he died I made them mine too. I grew up watching the English Premier League with him. I miss those days.

Mum presses a hand to my forehead. "Well, you don't feel particularly hot, so it's probably nothing serious. I think not eating before the game was a bad idea though, and all the extra work in high school must be exhausting you."

I nod.

"I'm sure it's nothing serious that sleep and then a big dinner can't fix."

I nod again. I wish she'd stop talking. I wish she'd go away.

Dad covers me with a blanket as Mum closes the blinds, instantly bringing a dark calmness to the usual bright white lounge.

"You'll feel much better afterwards," Mum adds, stroking my hair back and kissing my forehead.

I want to agree with this, I do. And I wish so hard

she was right. But the problem is I know that's not going to happen. I know because I've been wishing for these feelings to go away for a long time now – months. Wishing to wake up in the morning and feel normal, like when I used to itch to get out of the house and play football, to hang with Ted and the others at the park. Wishing that my schoolwork didn't feel so hard and that my body had more energy.

And I'm scared. I'm scared all the time. About everything but for no obvious reason. Getting over that fear every day uses up all my energy.

I stare at the artwork hanging on the wall above the sofa, watching the colourful dots and paint strokes in the shape of a turtle swirl and blend into one. Exhaustion comes for me quickly, and as I drowse, the heaviness leaves me and I force images into my mind of Fifi munching on her stick and her big brown eyes watching me expectantly for a game or a cuddle.

I wish I could be a dog: happy and calm, with no worries whatsoever.

And then I sleep.

3

It's so quiet, I easily hear the knock on the front door from all the way up in my room on the second floor, and I know it's Ted because it's his usual three quick raps. Plus, Ted always comes over on Saturday afternoons – it's one of the few times a week he gets a break from helping his mum at home; he can't even make every training session. His mum's a nurse and works long hours and double shifts, so sometimes he has to babysit his younger brothers.

I grip my phone tighter and look up at my white ceiling, wondering whether to go down and see him. I want to, I really do, but right now the shame is ripping its way through me, and I don't think I can ever face anyone ever again. I continue lying on my bed, feet crossed at the ankles, the mid-afternoon sun creeping into my room beneath the black blinds.

There's a light tap on my door and it opens. Dad pokes his head through the thin gap.

"It's Ted. Want to see him?" he whispers, thick eyebrows arched.

I pause, thinking about how gutted Ted will be. I touch the purple friendship band on my wrist, but then shake my head.

"Sure?" Dad asks.

I nod this time, and whisper, "Yeah, can you tell him I'm in the shower or sick or something and I'll call him later?"

Dad gives me a smile, pink lips stretching through his trimmed brown beard, a smile that makes me feel sad. "No probs." He closes my bedroom door quietly, and I hear his light footsteps padding down the carpeted stairs.

I let out a big breath and a few tears, realizing only now that my chest has tightened again. Not quite like it did back at football – it's never been that bad before.

I can't believe I didn't go down and see Ted. I regret it now, but I can't seem to muster the energy to chase after Dad or change my mind. My best mate of nearly six years, since our mums made us have a joint sixth birthday party with Kai too. He probably came over to see how I am, make sure I'm not sick after my football performance. And I know how much our Saturday afternoons together mean to him.

Hopefully Kai is with him. Kai's a better friend than me.

I shake off how irritated I feel with myself and look

back at my phone screen. I scroll through my PicRoll feed, sliding past the new memes and jokes and photos that match my interests. My parents – Mum mainly – finally gave in and let me have a phone for high school, since I walk there and back on my own now. It's not far, and loads of kids younger than me travel to school on their own. I know I should be grateful and appreciate the freedom. I can't believe they let me have a PicRoll account too, with parental settings of course, even if it was only because Ted's allowed one. But I have absolutely nothing to post today, nothing to tell anyone – the last time I posted anything was two weeks ago. I let my hand flop to my side and release a big sigh, a new surge of tears building behind my closed eyelids.

Poor Ted. Poor Mum and Dad.

I huff onto my side and shut my eyes, flinging my arm over my face, and my mind goes over and over what's happened today until I fall asleep again.

Dad parks and shuts down the engine of his truck, plunging us into a soft quiet. He looks across at me.

"All good?" he asks.

"Yeah, all good," I reply.

"Come on then, we haven't taken a bush walk together for ages."

Dad opens the door and hops out, and I copy, plopping two feet onto the gravel with a crunch. I close the truck door and check the small, square car park again – it's still empty except for Dad's truck. No one else here, thank goodness.

I shake my head at my silliness. The best thing about Hayden Lake National Park is that hardly anyone comes up here this early in the morning, other than old people and maybe a few runners.

The sun still sits fairly low, a yellow-white haze stretching from its core across the blue sky, and I have to admit that the world looks pretty Disney right now.

Dad comes round to my side and together our flip-flopped feet stroll side by side through the iron gate and onto the pathway that leads through the rainforest walk.

"Got the seeds for the ducks and swans?"

I pat my pocket, the paper bag crinkling beneath my palm. "Yup. And the cornflakes for me." I love snacking on dry cornflakes, something Grandad got me into.

Dad chuckles. "Nice. I'm surprised you're not full up from that porridge this morning."

After not eating much yesterday, I was starving.

It's warm already but the trees create a light-speckled roof above us and bring a coolness to my neck and face. The birds chirp their good mornings as we pass, flitting from branch to branch, and bushes and leaves rustle as unseen creatures scarper, probably thinking we're coming for them. As if we would. I love animals; Dad does too.

I suck in deep breaths, feeling pretty OK today after yesterday's embarrassing nightmare. Mum was up and out first thing today, working – she cuts hair for private clients some Sundays. Me and Dad were up early, so Dad suggested a walk and maybe a kickabout. I deliberately accidentally forgot the ball though, so a walk it is.

"So, you're feeling better today?" Dad asks, eyeing the path at his feet.

I nod. "Yeah." I say it with a weird hiccup laugh, like it's a joke. But who am I kidding?

I glance sideways and see Dad nod, sliding the long stick he keeps in the back of the truck through the leaves and rocks that border the bumpy path.

I'm clearly not kidding him, that's for sure.

"You know, it's OK if you want to talk about anything," he adds, tapping the stick on the base of a tree trunk. "I'm pretty good at listening."

It's true. Dad's a man of few words, as Mum calls him, which always leads to her telling everyone that's why they're so perfect for each other – chalk and cheese. I don't think I've ever heard Dad even raise his voice in all my life.

I suppose I could mention a few things to him now. After all, Mum isn't here to interrupt and take over the conversation, or tell me how I should feel. I nibble the inside of my bottom lip, not knowing what to say or where to even start. I don't want to upset Dad.

"I…" I run a hand through my floppy hair, a gentle breeze stroking my cheeks.

"No rush, mate. We've got a three-kilometre trek ahead of us." Dad grins and winks, scratching his beard.

I roll my eyes. Three kilometres and I already have the most achy legs in the whole of Queensland. Why did I agree to this again? Oh right, agreeing was a way to make up for yesterday's football "episode".

No, I don't think I can talk to Dad. I'm worried about how he'll react if he knows all the things going on in my head, and then he too will be ashamed of me, like Mum. If she is. It's so hard to tell with her. And anyway, I don't really know how to describe what I'm feeling or put my finger on what's wrong exactly.

I sigh and change the subject, scanning the thick rainforest stretching into the distance on either side of us and up ahead. "I texted Ted last night. They won yesterday."

"Oh yeah, what was the score?"

"Four–two. Nil–nil at half-time."

"Wow, busy second half. Who scored?"

I tell him, a nugget of annoyance flaring. I wish I'd been there to help my team. Wish I'd at least hung around to watch the Whales win and then had a lemonade at the clubhouse with some of the players and watched the under eighteens play their match after, like we normally do. But, to be fair, that result shows my team don't even really need me. Something I already know. It hurts, but I deserve it.

We walk on, a calmness between us as we chat about general stuff like TV shows, computer games or the different trees. The lake is probably about another five minutes away.

I spot something moving up ahead and my footsteps falter. I peek at Dad; he's noticed it too.

"What is it?" I ask, looking straight ahead again.

"I don't know."

We slow down, the trees seeming to hold their breath along with me, emptying the air completely. I squint and try to make out what it is. It's hard to see as the dark shape blends into the brown of the trunks and sticks. But I see it move. Just slightly, but definitely a movement.

My eyes widen. "Do you think it's a possum, or a koala even?"

Dad places his hand on my arm and raises his stick out in front of him. We creep forward, both of us careful not to scare it.

"Brush-turkey? Snake?" I know it's neither of those.

We inch closer. The fact it isn't running away is ringing all kinds of alarm bells. I'm not the most knowledgeable about native wildlife, but I do know most creatures will hide the minute they know there are predators approaching.

"I think it's injured," I whisper, a strange panic balling up in my throat. I cannot handle a nearly dead animal or bird. Anything like that would etch permanently into my brain and heart.

We're close now, maybe a few metres away, and then it shuffles again.

"It knows we're here," I say.

A small head lifts and I freeze completely.

It's a dog.

4

"Dad!" I grip my dad's hairy forearm, hands shaking.

"I see it, I see it," he says.

"What's it doing here?" I ask, standing still, eyes not blinking. I scan the area ahead, behind and deep into the trees for any signs of an owner. This park is not a good place for a dog, especially a small one like this.

"I don't know, but I think it's hurt. We need to be careful in case it's a stray or scared or something." Dad crouches down and I copy, and together – Dad a pace in front of me with his stick leading the way – we edge closer.

A faint whine reaches my ears and then another. It's definitely injured.

My heart melts. What could have happened for it to end up here?

"Dad, we need to help it." My voice is breathless.

I hate this. This dog … it doesn't look good. It's quivering as if it's freezing cold, and its face is filthy. In fact its entire coat, what's left of that anyway, is messy and covered in dirt. There are several bald patches breaking up short, matted, possibly brown fur; I can't tell its colour. One of its eyes looks completely closed, and one ear points up, the other pressed back against its head.

And I spot blood on its neck.

"It's been tied up. Look," Dad says, pointing at the thin tree trunk beside the dog.

He's right. There's grey rope tied around the trunk and the dog's neck – that's what's made it bleed, digging into its skin. I swallow, my stomach diving down into the depths of my body. "What should we do?" I ask, my voice super whispery, the words struggling to get past the shock wedged in my chest.

Dad doesn't answer straightaway, and when I look at him, I see the same well of emotion mirrored in his expression. He glances sideways at me and shakes his head, like he can't believe what he's seeing either.

He lets out a sigh, low and quiet but long – his composure sigh – and then squats. I park my butt on the stony ground beside him, my eyes drawn back to the little dog. It backs up, limping behind the tree it's tied to, like it thinks it's hiding from us or something. Its head is down and the shaking... Ugh, the shaking racks its entire scrawny body, all the way from its tiny paws to its one pointed-up ear. It makes me wonder if this is how I might have looked on the football pitch yesterday.

Dad pats my arm and I tear my eyes away. "Take a couple of photos, but quiet."

"Why?"

Dad shrugs. "Evidence, I guess. The poor thing is petrified, and we have no idea if it's aggressive."

I can't imagine that, but I nod, and gently, slowly, remove my phone from my pocket and type in the pass code. I raise it and zoom in on the dog. I can hardly keep my eyes on the screen, on this scared, skinny animal, as I snap a few pictures. My heart feels like it's been kicked.

"Someone's really mistreated…" I whisper, but the next words catch and die in my throat.

"I know, I know." Dad's shaking his head again, back and forth, as if that might help him process what's happening. He lays his stick on the ground and carefully removes his own phone from his pocket.

The dog whines again and a few tears trickle down my cheeks at what could be the saddest sound I've ever heard. It's crying. My hand brushes against my shorts, rustling the bag of cornflakes. I reach inside and pull the brown paper bag out, as quietly as I can, and place it on the ground in front of me.

"Dad, should I try to feed it? It's so skinny and bony,

it has to be hungry. It might let us get closer that way and then we can save it." There's no doubt in my mind that I have to save it.

Dad glances up from his scrolling. "Maybe. Give me a second. I'm looking to see what advice the internet gives about finding a lost dog."

"I don't think it's lost," I reply, my eyes flicking back to the bloodstained rope around the dog's neck and then to the deserted park.

"I know, I just…" He doesn't complete the sentence and he doesn't have to. I know he's as shocked as me.

We sit in silence for a little longer, as chirping, squawking birds and the breeze play together among the leaves and bushes. Ordinarily I like the sound, but right now it's loud and irritating and feels threatening. I work hard to block it all out, along with any thoughts of what might have happened to the dog, and instead focus on how I can help it, putting myself in its position and trying to understand how afraid it must feel. I know fear, but this is something else, and I feel silly to think I had problems. Right now, I want nothing more than to show this animal that not all people are bad, that it doesn't have to be afraid. That it can trust me.

I need to put my own worries aside.

"OK," Dad says. "I think … I think we need to see if we can approach it and maybe get it to a vet. It's

Sunday and I honestly don't know how long it would take for someone from the council or welfare league or whatever to come out and fetch it, and I don't even know if I want to go down that path." He looks up at the dog, which now sits, still partially hidden behind the tree trunk, its head lowered and back hunched, nose almost touching the ground. "I don't know how badly it's injured. Time might be all it has."

My chest squeezes like someone's gripped my heart and lungs, and it reminds me again of how I felt yesterday, but my determination ratchets. I need to help this dog.

"Should we try to feed it then?" I ask again.

Dad nods. "Yep, internet says to stay low, move slowly and use a calm voice. We can toss some small bits of food on the floor where it might be able to reach them and see how we go."

Unfolding the top of the paper bag, I remove a couple of cornflakes and place them in the palm of my hand and then some in Dad's palm. Then, crouched, we inch nearer. The dog doesn't even look up this time, just keeps on quivering and staring at the ground with its one open eye, uttering barely audible whimpers. We're only a metre away, maybe less now, and it's clear it's a boy dog. Dad reaches forward and places a cornflake on the ground. I do the same, and then we wait.

Using a soft and calm voice, I say, "Hey, mate, it's OK." I try to get my shaking under control. "Not all people will hurt you. I promise. Not all humans are bad. Look, we've got some yummy food. Well, not all that yummy. Cornflakes are better with milk and sugar, or golden syrup, that's my favourite, but you might like them like this. You don't look like you've eaten much in a while."

Dad and I share a look, and he smiles and nods for me to continue, and so I do. I keep talking, my eyes staring off to the side of the dog so as not to look menacing. I don't want to intimidate the poor thing. I tell the dog about other food he might like, about my favourite meals. About butter chicken and pilaf rice, roast potatoes and gravy, and meatballs in creamy mustard sauce. I rabbit on, gently and slowly, and then I see him move. Eyes flicking up to my hand, to my face. It's only a slight movement, but it's enough for me to know he's interested.

The dog's nose now wiggles in the direction of the cornflakes we dropped. I wish we'd brought something tastier – but then I didn't know we'd be rescuing a dog.

I hold my breath, watching him, waiting. He slides his front paws through the sticks and leaves, lifting his rump and standing on wobbly legs that won't straighten, as if his body is too heavy. Legs that are nothing more than bones and mangy fur. And this close I can see that the fur he does have is a mixture of black and brown, a few grey and almost gold tufts on his face and on the one ear sticking up. The dog comes right up to the cornflake, and I don't think I've ever sat so still in all my life as I wait. The only part of me I feel moving is my heart.

Come on.

The dog's head dips low and he snuffles the cornflake, scooping it up into his mouth.

"You're a good boy," I whisper.

A cheer releases inside my head, but as the dog tries to chew it, the cornflake falls out the side of his mouth. But he tries again, picking up the cereal and chewing, this time crunching it on the other side of his mouth and swallowing. I smile and give Dad the smallest nudge on his leg.

I carefully toss another cornflake on the ground beside the dog, talking again to him like he's an old friend, and though he cowers at first, he doesn't go back to his spot behind the tree. He uses his one open eye and nose to track the new cornflake and gobbles it up.

Dad and I throw more morsels to him, and after each time the dog swallows he looks at us expectantly through his one good, brown eye. The temperature's rising, sweat collecting on my back beneath my T-shirt, but the trees are big and crowded enough to keep the sun off us. The dog's still shaking, but I think less, more like shuddering and then stopping and then shuddering again.

I think he's starting to trust us.

And so I decide to try something new.

I talk some more as I pinch a cornflake between my finger and thumb. "I bet you'd like to meet Fifi. She's Jane's dog. Jane lives next door…" I shuffle closer, hand outstretched.

"Careful," Dad says, low and soft, hand on my shoulder.

"Jane's nice and Fifi is great fun." I wait, my arm straight, back of my hand resting on the scratchy ground. "She loves to play with sticks. Maybe we could play a game like that one day." The dog extends his neck, eye fixed on my palm. Nerves and excitement buzz under the surface of my skin. "I have lots of balls at home, so we could play fetch or…"

And the dog's rough nose and wet mouth touch my fingertips as he takes the cornflake.

A glimmer of happiness swells inside my body.

5

The dog lies beside me, the top of his head pressed against my knee. He absolutely stinks, but I've got used to it now. I have my hand on his head, the fur rough and spiky but soft in other spots. He took loads of bits of cornflakes from my hand, almost all of what I brought, until suddenly it was as if his legs gave out and he collapsed onto his tummy, head flopping down. He's breathing; I can see his bony chest moving in and out, up and down, and he's not shaking. I think he must be utterly exhausted. His good eye is shut now too, and I remain still and calm. Even though he might be sleeping, I don't stop talking.

"Dad will be back in a second," I tell him. "He's just run back to get some blankets or towels or whatever he can find in the truck to make you warm and comfortable, and then we'll get you to the vet." I swallow, studying his sunken ribcage and bloated belly, thankful Dad is fit and can run fast. "You're going to be OK," I say, sniffing as a few fresh tears fall.

I use my other hand to take some more pictures of him. The saddest part is, via the screen on my phone, I've been able to see the sores on his body in more detail and how his neck beneath the rope is all red and just horrible.

Through my hand on his head, I press all my good thoughts and energy past his fur and skin and into his body. Then I have a thought.

"You need a name." I cock my head to one side. "Yes, you definitely need a name." I rub my eyes and nose on my white T-shirt at the shoulder and think, glancing at the dog and at the trees around me. "Doug. Duggie. Georgie. Na ... Puff. Puffy?" That's how my eyes feel, but I don't think it's right for him. "Muck. Nah, that's rubbish. Erm ... One Eye? One Ear? Cornflake. That might work." And then a face pops into my mind and I know it's perfect. A smile curls the corner of my mouth and I let out a breath.

"Cliff." I nod, smiling wider. "Cliff the dog." I look down at him, at his tiny, skinny body and legs, his scuffed and cut paws, and his chest rising and falling. "What do you think of that for a name, buddy?" I ask him, wiggling my fingertip back and forth across his head. "Cliff. After my grandad because he was cool for an old man."

For some reason new tears form as I think of my grandad, but they don't feel like sad tears. A small surge of adrenaline bubbles in my chest and a laugh trickles out.

"Do you hear that? You're Cliff now, and your life is going to get better, I promise."

Footsteps scuff behind me, and I swivel the top half of my body as carefully as possible so I don't disturb Cliff. Dad jogs over, wads of material bundled in his arms, and I can tell he's trying to keep his footsteps light. He slows to a walk, a tiptoe, and then crouches beside me.

"How's he doing?" he asks, a little breathless. It was quite a distance back to the truck and he must have sprinted all the way there and back.

"OK, I think he's sleeping."

Dad presses a finger to his nose. "Gosh, he stinks." He swallows. "OK, not sure how we're going to do this. But first I've got to cut this rope." He unwraps a big pair of metal scissor things from the pile of dirty, dusty sheets he uses for work. Hard dried paint, mainly white, is splattered on the sheets, but they look softer than the stick-covered ground Cliff is lying on right now.

"Keep him as calm as you can, Matt," Dad says as he squats and snips at the middle of the rope. He cuts through it and the rope falls away. Cliff doesn't move an inch. "Wait, what's this?" I frown and watch him pick up a mucky piece of white paper from behind the tree Cliff was tied to. He turns it over in his hand and I see some words on it. Big letters in black marker.

'What does it say?" I ask.

Dad shakes his head and folds the paper up, putting it in his pocket.

"Dad?"

He rubs his forehead. "It says, *UGLY, SAD DOG. HE'S YOURS.*"

I screw up my face, anger and rage and disgust fighting for control. Words abandon me and they seem to have abandoned Dad too. We're frozen, processing how anyone could be so cruel. Then Dad seems to come to.

"Right, now we need to pick him up."

I stare at Cliff, wondering how much it's going to hurt him when I lift him. I imagine the pain in my own legs and body. "I'm not sure..."

"It's OK," Dad says. "We'll do it together."

I nod, and Dad lays out one of the sheets beside me. I shove my phone in my pocket and wipe at my eyes to clear the final horrified tears. I slide my friendship band as far up my arm as it will go.

"I'll slip my hands under his backside; you get his head and front legs, OK?" Dad says.

And we do it.

I wiggle my fingers until my hands are as far under

his bony body as I can get them and Dad does the same until our fingers are overlapped, and then we lift on a count of three, moving Cliff forward and placing him slowly and gingerly down onto the soft sheet. He's so light, so small and fragile, that it's easily done. But the fact he still doesn't move, barely even opens his eyes … I don't like it.

"Dad, we need to go." The panic is tensing in my gut. I can't let anything happen to Cliff. I promised him things were going to get better and I'm determined to keep to it.

"I know, son, I know." Dad wraps the blanket around Cliff and then he lifts him and places him in my arms. "Got him?" he asks.

"Yep," I reply, hugging the sheets to my chest with both arms, barely able to feel Cliff's weedy body inside them.

"OK, let's go."

Dad and I walk side by side at a fast pace, occasionally glancing at each other and then at Cliff. His little head pokes out of his cocoon and rests in the crook of my arm. "It's OK, Cliff, we're nearly there."

"Cliff?" Dad frowns and side-eyes me.

"Ah, yeah, I thought…"

I swallow, not sure how Dad will take it. Grandad was Dad's dad and I know he gets super sad when we talk about him. Sometimes I feel sad about it too – about Grandad not being here, about how upset Dad gets. Mum used to say we three were the most sensitive boys in the world, but she loved Grandad as well. She said he was more like a dad to her than her real one.

Dad grins and nods, eyebrows springing up. "I like it. Suits him."

I smile, relieved and even more convinced we were meant to stumble across Cliff today. I just hope we found him in time.

6

I hold Cliff tight the whole drive to the emergency vet. As it's Sunday, the closest one open today is about a twenty-minute drive away at Rosie's Beach, and I don't like to admit it, but I'm getting more and more worried about Cliff. Each and every minute I check under the sheet to make sure his chest is still moving, and again when Dad drives over a bump or brakes suddenly, a waft of Cliff's stench hitting me. There's a lot of traffic, with families headed to the beach and the shops and wherever else people go on their day off. I don't think there's a single muscle in my body that's relaxed right now.

Dad and I barely speak the entire drive, and he doesn't even turn on the radio, almost as if any noise might make Cliff more scared. But, right now, I don't think any of it would matter.

I stare at Cliff's little head, his snout and black nose and closed eyes, his pointy ear and his flat one. I can literally feel the tiredness releasing from his body every time he exhales. "Come on, Cliff," I whisper, my lips close to his face. "It's all going to be OK. I promise." I repeat it over and over, the words hardly audible even in my ears, but enough so it focuses the crazy headache of emotions and thoughts circling like vultures.

And then we're swerving off the main highway and into a small parade of shops. Dad parks up outside a glass-fronted shop with ROSIE'S BEACH VET on the green sign. There's a small store next door called ROSIE'S BEACH PET STORE. I feel like I'm having that out-of-body experience again, like at football. All sounds are buried and my vision feels sharp but slow at the same time. I can't collapse and vomit again. Not here, not with Cliff in my arms.

I have to keep it together.

Dad guides me out of the truck, and I try to move like I'm floating, so as not to disturb Cliff. "Nice and slow," Dad says, hands supporting the nest of sheets Cliff's inside. Someone opens the glass door, an older woman with curly brown and grey hair and a white jacket that's open at the front. She's wearing blue trousers, a white T-shirt and bright white Converse, and she has this smile on her face that's both reassuring and terrifying. She moves in a way that says she means business, that she's here to get the job done and nothing more.

"Mr Brown?"

"Yes, that's me," Dad replies.

"Great, thanks for calling ahead. We're ready for you. Come inside," she says, shaking Dad's hand and gesturing towards the clinic behind her. I float forward on my barely there legs, past a younger woman holding the door open for me, hair scraped back into a tight ponytail.

The older lady keeps talking. "I'm Sue and this is Melanie. So, you found this poor dog, huh?" Sue's voice is husky and direct, but there's an upbeat tone to her words at the same time.

Behind me I hear Dad filling Sue in on finding Cliff. I focus on Melanie and follow her past the small reception area, a row of plastic chairs, a desk, shelves filled with bags of animal food and bottles and pots of medicines and shampoos. Pop music plays faintly in the background. We veer off down a white-tiled corridor, and Melanie shoves open a door to her right and smiles at me, glossy pink lips wedged closed. This place is much bigger than it looks from the front.

"Just in here," she says, her small blue eyes focused on the bundle in my arms. "Put the little fella on the table there."

I do, carefully, so so carefully, placing the sheets and Cliff on the silver table top as gently as I possibly can. I'm trembling, terror and fear eating my insides alive. I slide my arms out from under him and place one palm on his head, exactly how I did back at Hayden Park.

"Will he be OK?" I ask, voice hollow, eyes not moving from Cliff's sleeping face.

"Well, let's do what we can for him, shall we?" Sue says, bursting into the cramped room and joining Melanie by the bench. She buttons up her jacket, washes her hands and slaps on some medical gloves. Melanie sidesteps and switches on a computer in the corner.

Dad steps in from the doorway and puts both his hands on my shoulders. I close my eyes, pressing all my wishes and hopes into Cliff's tiny head. "Come on, Cliff," I whisper. "Come on."

"If you two can wait outside, please," Sue says, unravelling Cliff from his soft shell. "I'll come out soon and update you, OK?" She shoots another of her terrifying toothy smiles at me.

Dad guides me away as Melanie and Sue start chatting, exchanging words and directing others at Cliff, most of which don't register fully in my brain. I stare over my shoulder at Cliff until the door closes and we're plunged into the silence of the stark white hallway. Dad sideways hugs me with both arms.

"It's OK, he'll be OK," he says, fingers gripping my shoulder.

"But will he?" I ask, my voice catching. I appreciate Dad being here, but sadness and worry overwhelm me more than any other emotion, and I can't relax into his embrace.

Dad sighs as we both sit down on the blue plastic chairs in reception. "I don't know. But we can hope and wish, right?"

I nod and bury my face in my hands, and Dad pulls me in again for another hug. I let some of my tension out and lean into his red T-shirt, soaking in the smell of his deodorant.

Come on, Cliff. Come on.

He has to be OK.

We sit and sit, and wait and wait, my butt going numb on the horrible hard chair, flipping the pages of magazines, scrolling through our phones. Dad texts Mum, but since she's at work we know she won't reply yet. PicRoll shows the usual stuff: Joseph posting pictures of himself at football and at the park with his mates and the usual followers, boasting about the win yesterday. He doesn't mention me and what happened. Thankfully. As the time passes, I do all I can not to look outside into the bright, blue world, at the cars and people charging by like life is the best thing ever. I focus on the radio playing in the background and read the words on the animal food bags over and over.

Shoes squeak on tiles, announcing someone's arrival, and Sue appears, striding heavily round the corner into reception. "Mr Brown," she says to both me and Dad. We rocket to our feet at the same time. Though her voice sounds confident, bright even, my gut is twisted like a rope.

"How's Cliff?" I blurt.

Sue grins and raises her thick eyebrows. "What a great name! I think he's going to need a lot of TLC, quite a long road to recovery ahead, but I'm confident he'll be fine."

And then I breathe. The biggest, longest breath I've ever taken, and flop forward, hands on my knees. The tightness releases in my chest and a laugh bursts out unexpectedly.

Dad pats me on the back.

"Yes, despite his appearance he doesn't appear to have anything terribly wrong with him. No broken bones or bites or diseases. Just a flea problem, malnourishment, dehydration, an eye infection, and a few nasty sores we can easily treat," Sue says.

Dad eyes me for a second and then turns back to Sue. "What happens now?" he asks.

I straighten up and chew the inside of my cheek, sliding my friendship band round and round my wrist. "Can we take him home?" I ask, my eyes shooting to Dad.

"Well, there are a number of things we have to do first," Sue replies, eyes thinning, "but we're going to have to keep him in for a few days first, monitor him, make sure his sores are healing and run a few blood tests. Feed him up!"

"Blood tests? What for?" I ask.

"Just precautionary. Not knowing where he's from means we have no medical history, so it's important we rule out anything life-threatening or possibly contagious."

I swallow and nod. So not completely in the clear yet.

Sue's expression softens and her eyes crease in the corners. "We'll know soon enough." She wanders behind the reception desk and sits. "My guess is he's been severely neglected, left outside to fend for himself until his owners have decided to move on or get rid of him."

"We did find him with a note..." Dad starts, and I see him glance at me. "But, basically it confirms he wasn't wanted. We have the note if you need it."

The words on the note scream out in my brain.

Sue continues, "Yes, I can keep that on file. So sad. People are shocking, aren't they? But with some food in his belly and a bit of love, I think he'll recover and live a very happy life. Even though he has no microchip or traceable owners, there are procedures, however..."

"What?" I shake my head, mouth falling open.

"In this situation, we have to contact the council and pound, who then list the dog in their database in case his owners are looking for him. But, since he has no ID, that will only be for three days, and then he can be put up for adoption."

"But his owners clearly mistreated him," Dad says, obviously with the same thoughts rushing through his mind as mine.

I can't believe this.

"It's procedure, I'm afraid. But anyway, I've been in this job for over thirty years and in my experience of cases like this the owners rarely come forward." She winks and my heart calms a beat. Sue may be a bit frightening but I trust her. "You're thinking of keeping him, are you?"

I glance at Dad, my eyes wide, pleading – pathetic probably – and then I nod once to Sue, biting my bottom lip. I know if it was only up to Dad he'd let me bring Cliff home. But we've got to get past Mum first, which means more rules and expectations than every teacher at Whaleview High School have combined.

Dad brings a loose fist to his lips and clears his throat into it. "It's something for us to discuss."

Sue raises her bushy eyebrows at Dad, and my mind screams at me to speak up, but the words won't come. Anger is all I feel, at this whole situation, at Cliff's evil owners.

"Listen, I know people at the council and pound," Sue says, "so let me have a talk with them. Maybe we can figure out a way for Cliff to avoid any time in the shelter as I doubt he'll cope. He'll be here for three days anyway." She smiles at me and I don't find it as terrifying as before. "At some point there will be the subject of money to discuss, but now I will need you to fill in some paperwork, please." Sue shakes the computer mouse and starts typing, while Dad leans on the blue-speckled counter.

"Have a seat, son," he says to me. "I'll be as quick as I can, OK." He turns back to Sue and they talk in low voices.

I spin away and stomp over to the row of seats, silent, thinking about Cliff, about this whole unfair situation. My stomach is in knots. I could be about to walk out of here and never see him again.

I can't let that happen. I can't.

I promised Cliff his life would get better. And I need him.

I feel so powerless to do anything, to fight for what I want. Like at football yesterday. I didn't want to play, should have spoken up before the game, said I couldn't do it. But, even though I'm so afraid of what's going to happen every day of my life at the moment, I'm also scared of letting everyone down, of people being annoyed with me.

Still, I promised Cliff. I said I would protect him. Am I letting him down too?

My head is such a mixed-up mess.

I sink lower in the chair, my body weighing a million tons. Maybe walking away is for the best, now that I think about it. I'm probably not the right person for the job. I'm not the right person for much lately; I can't even make it through a whole football game, so why would I be any good at caring for a dog? Mum's probably right. I should listen to her more often.

My heart plummets, and I fold my arms and grit my teeth. What is the actual point of me? Someone else should have found Cliff today.

7

I lean on the kitchen island, the hard, black stone benchtop digging into my hip, and take the last gulp of the chocolate milkshake Mum made me. Stevie Wonder songs play from the docking station where her phone sits. I stand beside Dad, who sits at the island on the wooden bar stool, heel tapping against the footrest as he tells Mum about us finding Cliff and what happened. It's only 2 p.m., and Jane's coming over for roast dinner soon, but this day feels like it's been going on for an eternity.

I'm so tired.

"Poor doggie," Mum says, switching on the gas to boil some veggies. The kitchen smells of Sunday roast meat and potatoes, and though it's delicious, I don't feel in the least bit hungry. I haven't eaten since breakfast and my tummy feels weird, but I don't want to think about that now. I yawn and lay my head on my folded arms on the benchtop, exhaustion wiping me off my feet like a sliding tackle.

"And the vet said she'd let you know how he goes?" Mum asks.

"She did," Dad answers, flipping the page of his newspaper.

"Aww, well, I hope he finds a nice new home when he's better."

My eyes meet Dad's for a brief moment before he looks back at the paper, his expression not giving anything away. My stomach flips.

"We were thinking, actually," Dad starts, eyes fixed on the page, "that maybe Cliff could come and live with us."

It's like a black hole has sucked the air out of the room. Even Stevie Wonder's voice seems to have quietened. I wait, eyes wide and fixed on Mum's back, on the vertical stripes of her blue-and-white vest top. The boiling water bubbles loudly, angrily in the pan, steam rising in wafts.

Mum turns and faces us, head shaking.

"We? We were thinking?" she says, eyebrows raised at me. "And it's that simple, is it?"

"He doesn't have a microchip or anything so if no one comes forward in three days to claim him, we can adopt him," Dad explains. "Sue said she'd do the best she can for him and us."

I lift my head and nod. "We'd be able to give him

a nice warm home and lots of love – that's what the vet said he'll need – I don't think he's had much of that so far." I try to keep any desperation out of my voice, but it's seeping in regardless.

She scratches her forehead with her long pink nails and shakes her head again. "I've said before that I don't want a dog. They're hard work. I don't need that in my life."

Dad pauses and smooths out the paper flat on the bench top. "This is a bit different though, Nat," he says.

"Is it? How?" Mum flings a tea towel over her shoulder and folds her arms.

"Because we found him," I reply.

"And?"

"I think we were meant to find him."

It sounds silly saying it out loud, and I can guess what Mum's going to say next.

"Honestly, Matty." She looks to the ceiling. "You were just in the right place at the right time. Or wrong time. I don't know. We don't have the time between us to dedicate to a dog, especially one that comes with so much baggage."

"We do! And I'll give all the money in my bank account to pay for his vet bills," I exclaim, instantly regretting it. But I'm irritated that Mum still treats me like a baby. Why do her rules have to be the ones we all live by? Why won't she let me grow up and prove I can be responsible?

"Vet bills? We have to pay for the vet bills?" Her eyes bore into Dad's skull. "And how expensive is that?" she adds, her voice rising.

"We'll talk about the money another time. Calm down, son," Dad says quietly to me.

I bite the inside of my cheek, a scream bubbling up underneath my skin.

"Nat, please. We have a comfortable house and I know Matthew would spend all the spare time he has with the dog."

Mum lets out a sharp laugh. "What spare time? He's at school Monday to Friday, does football training three nights a week and sometimes two games at the weekend and other than that he's with Ted. That doesn't leave much spare." She spins back to the veggies, banging pans as she drains them off at the sink in a cloud of steam – half of which is probably coming from her.

Dad opens his mouth to respond but I get in there first. "I don't want to go back to football."

Again the black hole slurps up the air like it's a delicious meal, freezing Mum and Dad in the wake of my words. Maybe this wasn't the right time, but I can't go back to football. I can't. I don't want to play and I don't even want to talk about it. I just want it all over.

Mum doesn't say anything, still, her silence is all the anger she needs to show. Instead she clatters plates and bowls about and starts dishing up dinner.

"Can you carve the meat, Brian?" she asks without facing Dad. "Jane will be here soon."

Dad stands, pats and squeezes my forearm, then immediately does as she asks. Why hasn't he said anything? Why hasn't either of them said anything?

I need to know what's happening with Cliff.

"So, can Cliff come and stay?"

"I'm not talking about it any further and you will be going back to football," Mum retorts. "We've already paid this year's fees."

Anger ripples its way to the surface and I slam my palms down on the bench. Mum and Dad both whip around. My breaths come fast and I can feel the burning in my cheeks, matching that of my stinging palms. I never get angry. Never disrespect my parents like this. I'm losing control.

"That'll do, thank you," Mum says, her face red. "Now go and lay the table before you find yourself in more trouble than you want."

A tear trickles from my eye as the anger fades, just like that, and I leave, shoulders drooped, head heavy. But I don't stop at the dining table. I don't grab any cutlery from the drawer, and I don't get the salt and pepper from the larder. I keep walking, dragging my sad, pathetic self through the hall towards the front door and then up the stairs. All the way up to the second storey, to my bedroom, and by the time I get there, I've got just enough energy left to open and close the door before falling into a heap on the floor.

I bury my face in the grey carpet and cry quietly, eyes closed, my head pounding the worst headache I've ever had.

By the time Dad comes up to my room, I have no emotions left and don't even open my eyes. He opens the door and crouches beside me, saying a few words. He's going to keep my dinner in the oven and will keep working on Mum – maybe even Jane will help with that – and then he leaves.

Why isn't anyone telling me off for getting so angry? I'm such a burden on their lives. I'm a terrible, miserable son, a let-down on the football pitch, and I can't even be the one to offer an abandoned dog a new home. I'm useless.

I wake up in my bed a while later, my door ajar, and am aware right away of the sound of Mum and Dad's voices. Maybe that's what woke me. Mum's is raised and Dad's is that usual deep rumble. I blink open my eyes slowly to see moonlight trickling in under the blinds.

"Oh, for goodness' sake, Brian. That's not it."

I take a few deep breaths and listen harder.

"But you lost your dad. You had a reason to feel down."

Dad rumbles a reply. I wish I could hear what he's saying. I think about opening the door, creeping downstairs, but I'm too tired.

"He's a child. Children don't get depressed," Mum says.

Depressed?

Are they talking about me?

Dad's saying something else.

"Matthew has a great life; he has everything he wants," Mum says. "Right now, he's just tired and overwhelmed, what with all the extra schoolwork and getting used to high school and his body is growing fast. That's it. He'll get through it."

Dad thinks I'm *depressed*?

Their conversation fades as they move away from their bedroom door.

It doesn't make sense. Mum's right. I've never heard of kids getting depression. It's an adult thing. Dad had to see someone after Grandad died two years ago, and Jane once told us that the only thing that rescued her from depression after her husband John died was her garden. Soldiers get depressed; people who've been in accidents or seen terrible things get depressed. Not kids, and definitely not kids who have everything.

My ears home in as Mum wanders across the hallway and back again.

"Listen, I'll think about the dog, OK, but no promises."

Yeah, right. Mum "thinking about it" means nothing, never, not happening.

I sigh and rub my eyes. They feel swollen and sore. I stretch over and lift my phone from my bedside table. It's 6.48 p.m. Wow. I slept for hours. But I still feel tired and my body hurts. I missed dinner and Jane coming over. She'd have been excited to talk to me about Cliff, I just know it.

I open my phone and slide through the photos of Cliff. My tummy tightens as I look at the sores on his skin and his rib bones visible and sticking out through his fur, at the memory of him whining and shaking. Poor guy. I'm confident his owners won't be tracked down; and even if they are found, they wrote a note telling whoever to take him because he's ugly and sad.

Before my anger at Mum and Cliff's owners builds into an inferno again, my phone vibrates in my hand. Ted's calling. I should answer it, chat to him and tell him about Cliff. He loves dogs. But I don't. I let it ring and ring until the message bank kicks in.

I sigh, guilty.

I text him.

> **Me:** Hey mate. Sorry, something wrong with my phone. Can't answer any calls.

> **Ted:** Nightmare. What's up?

> **Me:** Not much. You?

> **Ted:** About to play *Jungle Warfare* with Kai if you want to join?

I look up at my computer on my desk and nibble the inside of my cheek. I haven't played *Jungle Warfare* for days – another of my once-favourite things that no longer seem as fun. Anyway, I can't be bothered to set it up right now, with my headache throbbing away.

> **Me:** Can't. Mum's got some family evening planned. Ugh.

> **Ted:** LOL. No worries. See you at Kai's dinner thing tomorrow.

I freeze, heart diving to the pit of my stomach.

It's Kai's birthday tomorrow.

I forgot.

But now I remember. He had family stuff this weekend, with his dad and his dad's new wife, and the only time he could do anything with us – Ted and me, his supposed-to-be mate – was after school on Monday. I already bought a gaming voucher and card for him.

How could I have forgotten all this?

Ted: Should be fun.

It should be.

Last year we went to the dive boards in Southlands, where they held the World Championships the year before. It was such a laugh. It feels like way more than a year ago though, so much has changed.

Me: Yeah, definitely.

Ted: Hope you feel better.
See you at school.

Me: Capture some beasts for me.

Ted: 😂😂

I toss my phone to one side and release a long breath, wondering why and even how I forgot about

Kai's party. We're all about to turn twelve: Kai, then Ted, then me, our final birthday before we're teenagers. I'm surprised at myself for being so unthoughtful.

Way to go, best mate of the year.

There's a light tap on my door, and Mum opens it and steps into my room. "Hey, Matty," she says.

"Hey," I reply, dragging my aching body to a sitting position. I lean back against the wall, tensing up, prepared to hear the worst about Cliff not being allowed to live here.

She tiptoes across the carpet and sits on the bed beside me, running a hand through her long brown ponytail. I smell her perfume, flowery like Jane's yard, but interspersed with remnants of the roast dinner she cooked – that I didn't eat. She then fiddles with her wedding ring, twisting the gold band round and round her finger. I nibble my cheek again, on the same piece of raised skin, waiting for her to speak, but then decide to go first.

"Sorry about earlier," I say.

She tilts her head to the side, brown eyes peering into mine, and then presses a hand to my forehead before stroking my hair back, like she usually does. "That's OK, my love. It must have been stressful seeing that dog like that. You're emotional and sensitive and I love that about you."

I nod and smile back at her smile.

Mum goes back to fiddling with her ring. "Hopefully all the sleep you've had this weekend is helping. Your body clearly needs it." She sighs. "Listen, I don't really know what's going on with football at the moment, with you ... but I don't want to see you so unhappy. Is it school, is it friends, a girl?"

I cringe and shake my head.

"Anyway, I've had a chat with Stu just now and he's happy for you to take next week off training as long as you do some fitness at home, OK? And your first league game of the season next weekend is a bye anyway."

A pressure unravels in my chest. There's no game next weekend. I don't have to let anyone down. "OK, thanks." If anything, Stu's probably relieved I won't be at training too.

"Hopefully with a week off you can get back to your usual self, right?" She raises her eyebrows.

"Right." Maybe a week off is what I need, though the pressure returns to my chest at the thought of going back to training.

"And, I'm not promising anything, but I will have a think about the dog."

I can't stop the full-on smile this time. "Thanks, Mum."

She runs a hand through my hair again. "There's

some serious responsibility involved with keeping a dog, probably even more with this dog, and we have a lot to discuss. Don't get your hopes up, OK?"

"No, I won't. But you'll love Cliff when you meet him." At least I hope she does.

She gives me an eye roll, but I can tell it's a fun one as she lets out a breathy laugh. "Perhaps when the vet calls, we can – all three of us – go and see him. Is that fair?"

I nod and thank Dad and Jane in my head for whatever they said to talk Mum this far round.

"Right," she says, standing, straightening out her blue, silk pyjama bottoms. "Come down and have some food, please. You need food. And then it's time to sort your bag and uniform for tomorrow." She starts to leave, throwing words to me over her shoulder. "I know the first months at high school can be daunting, but you'll settle."

"Yeah, I know."

"And I hope you've done your homework. First parent consultations are coming up … soon, right?"

With a pretend scared face, she shuts the door and I grin, only for it to fall away quickly as the door clicks closed. Ugh, parent consultations. And ugh, homework. I had some worksheets in Maths and Science to do and haven't done any of it. I tried, I did, but I couldn't concentrate. I always did my homework at primary school, but for some reason I can't find the motivation now.

I'm going to be in so much trouble.

Maybe tomorrow I'll feel better, and then I can do my homework in break. But not now.

I close my eyes and soon fall back to sleep.

8

I let my bag fall from my shoulder onto the floor and drop into my seat next to Ted, as the rest of the boys and girls in my form class pile into the room around me, talking and shouting and finding their seats like always.

But for me, today doesn't feel like always.

"Hey, man, you didn't come for a kickabout on the field this morning. You still feeling ill?"

"Yeah, still pretty rough." It's not a lie. I ache all the way from my neck down to my knees. Maybe it *is* growing pains. Dad said he used to be in tons of pain when he was my age. Explains all the sleeping, too – and Mum's adamant it's a mixture of this and starting high school.

But my excuse is also part lie because I deliberately walked to school slowly this morning to avoid the normal kickabout. I didn't feel like it and I'm running out of excuses. I was so pleased last year when I found out Ted and Kai would be in the same form class as me, and Joseph wasn't, but seeing them every morning now feels like an effort. I force myself to smile and join in, when all I really want to do is sit quietly alone in my thoughts. I barely recognize myself any more.

I wrap my headphones around my phone and put it in my bag. "How was *Jungle Warfare*?" I ask, though I already know the answer as I saw Ted and Kai's videos uploaded onto PicRoll earlier.

"Oh man, it was awesome. We got infiltrated by beasts and were separated in Jungle 5. Dude, I was so spooked." Ted looks towards the classroom door. "Here comes the winner!"

I look up too and see Kai wandering between the rows of chairs and tables, arms outstretched like he's just scored a goal. My mouth quirks up on one side. Kai is so dramatic.

"Morning, losers," he says, high-fiving Ted and then me.

"Happy birthday," I say, leaning back in my chair and crossing my legs at the ankles. "Good weekend?"

"Top weekend. Spent the whole time at my dad's. Him and Flick took me go-karting and rock-climbing. Oh man, it was so cool."

Flick is Kai's dad's new wife but Kai lives with his mum.

Kai plonks down in his seat on the other side of

Ted. "You feeling better? Ted said you lost it at football on Saturday."

My belly clenches. *Lost it*. Nice.

"I never said lost it," Ted says to me, raising his palms in surrender. "Honest."

Kai smacks me lightly on the back of the head with his ruler. "He did. He totally did."

"I didn't," Ted says, honesty shining in his dark brown eyes.

"That's cool," I say, rubbing the back of my head. Ted's probably the only one who wouldn't say I lost it.

"Anyway, you can't be ill because tonight is birthday night! Banging Burgers here we come!"

A rush of heat burns across my skin, throbbing in my neck. "I hope I'll be OK," I say, clearing my throat even though there's nothing to clear apart from the lie. "Shouldn't really be here at school, to be honest."

I avoid Ted's gaze, totally aware that he's frowning in my direction, probably seeing right through me.

"Oh man, you have to come, it's our favourite place. It's going to be ... epic."

Kai whispers the last word as Ms Grassop enters the room, long black ponytail swinging side to side and heels clipping on the tiles. She looks like a horse in a showjumping contest, and Kai makes a quiet *clip-clop* sound with his tongue. The entire class settles down, green-checked Whaleview High shirts and dark green shorts shifting into seats and scraping chairs.

"Thank you, 7F, much appreciated," she says, placing her brown leather bag onto the table along with armfuls of paper.

Ugh, looks like another test.

Or more homework.

Butterflies swarm in my tummy.

"We'll do the roll and then move straight into today's test. As I call out your names, I would like you to be doing two things…"

She barks out her instructions and my stomach drops. As kids around me rustle in their bags, removing their homework books and passing around the test papers, I sink further into my seat. I have no homework to hand in and haven't done any revision. I'm no Maths genius, but my brain doesn't even know what today's test is going to be about. Why can't I remember? I was at school every day last week.

Ted elbows me and I startle, taking the pile of tests from him, removing the top one and passing the pile on to Bryony Black who sits in front. She's smart; maybe I could see some of her answers over her shoulder.

"Homework?" Ted whispers to me.

I shake my head. "Didn't feel well enough to do it."

What an excuse. I want to eye roll at myself.

I once again avoid looking at Ted.

Ms Grassop gets through the roll and we start working on the test. We have one hour which will take us up to morning break. After turning over the first page and scanning through the questions, I'm about ready to give up. It's like all previous Maths knowledge has left me. *Poof!* Sucked from my brain by that same black hole that attacked last night. Probably the same one that's been sucking all the important things I'm supposed to remember from my mind lately.

Which immediately makes me think about Kai's party later. And I don't want to think about that.

So I refocus and write a few things down with my pencil, rubbing them out, and then writing something else. I'm sure I know more about algebra than this, or at least enough to make an attempt at half these questions, but the emptiness in my head is the loudest whirring siren and it's making all the knowledge scarper into the darkest corners.

I sit and I try and I sit and I try.

I can't do this.

The black hole in my head drifts down, down, into my chest and my heart and my stomach, and I'm transported back to the football pitch on Saturday. Nope. Can't collapse like that, not here in the classroom.

What is wrong with me?

And then Ms Grassop clears her throat and announces time's up.

I flip my paper over, eyes drooping and tiredness sweeping over me again like a massive tidal wave of weighted emotions.

Well, that's something else to add to the failure list. Parent consultations are going to suck.

My teacher talks, but her words are slurring together in monotone. I place my hand to my head, in part because my head hurts, but also to block out Ted staring at me. I notice my other hand shaking and quickly hide it in my lap, training my eyes on my pencil lying crooked on the white desktop.

I answered about five questions out of fifty. All the pencils of the other kids were scribbling like there was no tomorrow. But not mine.

The bell goes for break and I realize I've been gritting my teeth so hard my jaw aches. I stretch my mouth wide open as I heave my bag up from under the desk and onto my shoulder.

"Hey, Matt, you coming to tuckshop?" Ted asks, packing away his stuff.

"Sure." I follow him out the classroom. He yawns and stretches his arms above his head. He looks tired and I guess he's been helping his mum this weekend with the cleaning and gardening and stuff. Ted's dad doesn't live at home with him and his younger brothers; he flew back up north about six years ago, a bit like how Kai's dad lives in another home with his new wife and Kai's baby half-sister an hour away in the city. I can't imagine how that must be, family all broken up and separated. I can't imagine a life where Dad doesn't live at home with us. Dad's the calm our house needs – the calm *I* need.

We pile through the corridors, kids thundering back and forth, charging off in every direction. My head stays down, watching my black shoes, mainly to avoid Joseph and his gang, but also because it feels too heavy to lift.

We make it to the tuckshop unscathed, and I join the melee of bodies waiting in some sort of line to be served, jostling, laughing and yelling. All enjoying life like it's the best thing ever. I'm sure I used to be like this. When did it change?

Ted and Kai are discussing what they're going to order tonight, but I'm struggling to keep up. My head's pounding again.

I tap Ted on the shoulder. "I'm going to the toilet."

Ted fixes me with his eyes, and I don't miss the pause before he answers, "Cool. Want me to get you anything?"

"Yeah, grab me a bag of crisps," I reply, shoving

a five-dollar note in his hand. "Get yours and Kai's out of that too." I back away, through the bodies of kids behind me, hoping my gesture will keep Ted off my back.

"Cheers, mate," I hear him reply as I turn, head down again, and elbow my way past a wall of green uniforms. I stride quickly past classrooms and pockets of kids, legs feeling numb, to the toilet block at the other end of the purple quad, the outside area reserved for year sevens and eights. It's usually way quieter than anywhere else – and right now I long for some quiet. I need to be where no one sees me.

My footsteps are so heavy, like I'm lugging bricks strapped to my shoes across the concrete playground. I'm taking so long to reach the toilets. My stupid legs aren't going anywhere near as fast as I want them to, and I snarl, angry at them and at myself.

"Feeling better?"

The words are directed at me, I know it.

I close my eyes briefly and then peer right, towards the voice. It's Joseph and his mates playing handball, a group of girls surrounding them.

Facing forward, I give a thumbs-up but don't bother to reply. This group are just bullies. I mean, Joseph has never picked on me directly, but after yesterday he's got plenty of ammunition.

I expect to receive an insult or some cutting nasty comment about me embarrassing myself on Saturday, but I don't. I do hear Joseph speak again but not the actual words, and as I reach the toilet door, pressing my hands against the chipped purple paint, I glance over at him. He's looking at me, no expression on his face at all, so I don't respond, just shove open the door and go straight into a cubicle.

Tossing my bag to the floor, I flip the toilet lid down and sit, dropping my head into my hands, elbows taking all the weight on my knees. I inhale, not even caring about the gross toilet smell. And I keep inhaling, one deep breath after another, but it isn't calming me down at all.

The tears are there, right there, behind my eyes, in my throat. I squeeze my eyes closed and clench my teeth.

No! I can't do this now. Tears at school would be the end of me.

But maybe that's all I deserve.

I can't do this.

I grit my teeth harder and growl in the back of my throat, shoving back the tears, pressing my fingertips onto my eyelids.

After a minute or more, I wipe at my eyes. I have to go home. I can't cry at school and I have Science with more homework due that I haven't done, then French and Sport still to go. I'll no doubt embarrass myself in all of those lessons too, even though French and Sport are what I'm best at. Maybe I don't deserve to go to my favourite lessons if I can't handle any of the others.

It would be better for my friends if I went home – especially as it's Kai's birthday. What fun am I to have around?

I reach into my bag and pull out my phone, planning to give Dad a call to ask – beg – him if I can go home.

I switch it on and see a message. It's from Dad.

Dad: Vet called. Cliff is doing great and we can visit tonight! Maybe take Mum?

For the first time today, I feel lighter and immediately text Dad back.

Me: Cool. Can you come and get me from school now? I'm not feeling well.

I wait, hoping Dad's got his phone on him and he's working locally. The bell sounds, which means kids will be heading back to class now. There's no way I can join them.

I stare at my phone screen, willing Dad to respond. My phone vibrates in my hand.

Dad: Be there in 20. Sick bay pick-up?

Me: Yes, thanks Dad.

The tears are creeping back, snot rushing to my nose and heat burning my face, but I fight it all off with a rough shake of my head.

I'm falling apart.

I hoist my bag onto my shoulder, the effort making me topple forward into the back of the cubicle door. With another deep intake of breath, I trudge from the safety of the graffiti-ridden toilet and head across the quad towards the office. The emptiness of the playground should make me pleased, pleased that Joseph isn't looking at me, but for some reason it fills me with this weird sadness.

Poor Kai. Poor Ted.

And poor Dad. All excited that we get to go and see Cliff later, still working on getting Mum to agree to let us keep him. And then me, disturbing him at work and making him come get me.

What kind of loser sits in a toilet all break, trying not to cry? What kind of loser doesn't want to hang with one of his best mates on his birthday?

Me.

9

I'm back in bed under my covers, a place I seem to spend so much of my time lately, but I always feel safer here. My bed means I get to rest my body, and my bedroom means I get to lie in the quiet. And it means I can't upset my friends and family or ruin anyone's life.

My window's open; a light wind rustles leaves outside in the warm March air and lifts my blind as it drifts into my room. It brings with it the smell of flowers from Jane's yard, honeysuckle the main one I recognize.

Dad's downstairs doing some paperwork. He wasn't cross with me or anything when he picked me up; part of me kind of wished he had been, though I have no idea why I'd wish that. I feel bad anyway. He was so excited, or at least trying to get me excited about seeing Cliff later. And I *am* excited. Truly. But I'm also tired and feeling guilty about Kai.

I shake the feelings and thoughts from my head. I haven't been eating properly and Kai's mum would totally waste her money on me by buying burgers and chips and cake, and Banging Burgers plays dance music way too loud which would be a bad idea for my headache. This way, it works out best for everyone.

I can't sleep, even though I'm tired, so I'm finishing the Science homework that was due in today. At least I've been *trying* to answer the questions about acid rain but every time I read one of the questions, my brain can't make any sense of the words. I don't get why I'm finding it so hard. A flash of impatience has me gritting my teeth and grabbing the book. With a growl, I launch it across my bedroom so it *thunks* against the back of my door. It lands closed on the carpet.

Tears prick at my eyes but I screw up my face, tensing my muscles until they hurt. *No more pathetic tears.* With wide eyes I look round my room, at my bookshelves, trying to think of something to do that will take my mind off homework – off my life. My football trophies and medals take up the top two shelves and I have a collection of football books and DVDs, football freestylers and biographies and the history of great players and goals, which sit beside my *Jungle Warfare* guides. My eyes linger on the player of the year trophy I got last season – a gold football sitting on top of a gold base and my name engraved on the plaque.

Why can't I be the same Matt I was back then?

Maybe I should take it down.

Fifi yaps outside and I sit up on my bed. I duck under my lowered blind and look out the window. She's right up at the end of Jane's back garden, head in the bushes with the big red flowers at the border, barking crazily at something, probably a lizard or bird, that's hiding in there. Dad's out there now too, standing on our side of the fence and chatting with Jane.

I watch Fifi's tiny paws scuffing and disturbing the dark brown bark Jane's laid around her plants, and I smile as Jane shuffles in her velvet slippers across the lawn that weaves through the large flowerbeds on both sides of her yard.

"Fifi. Fifi! Come on, come away. Leave it alone." Jane scoops Fifi into her arms and snuzzles her face, and Fifi licks Jane's cheek and nose. "You little pickle," she says, smiling, and then she glances up at my window.

It's too late to duck out of sight so I wave. She waves one of Fifi's paws at me, and Dad turns round too, shading his eyes from the sun. "You OK, Matty?" Jane calls up, using one hand to shelter her eyes from the sun too.

"Yeah, not too bad, thanks," I say.

"Aww, you poor young chappy. Well, you can always come over and see Fifi if you want. She'll make you feel better." Jane looks down at Fifi.

I smile. "Thanks, Jane."

"Just yell if you need us," Dad says.

Jane waves Fifi's paw at me again and stands with Dad, facing away from me and towards the small field that backs on to our yards. I walk on my knees across my bed and lie on my side, head sinking into the squishy pillows, and I let the darkness and quiet settle over the room again.

I force Cliff's face into my head. I might get to see him later.

Maybe him being in the house, being my friend, will make me feel happier. Fifi sure does make Jane smile. If I can concentrate on making him better, I'll have something to occupy my mind. Mum always says most things can be controlled with mind over matter and you only have to distract yourself and stay positive and it will improve. She's right. And Cliff will be the positive.

I glance at my football clock, at the hands that are footballer's legs and boots, hanging above my desk that sits there all neat and tidy, laptop closed. It's 2.35 p.m. School will be finished in ten minutes and Mum will be home just after four. Dad said we'd head over to see Cliff straightaway before the vet closes.

I lean over and grab my phone. My fingertip hovers over the on button, pausing because I know there'll be messages from my friends wondering where I am and if I'm going tonight.

I turn it on, deliberately ignoring the notifications, and again flick straight to the photos I snapped of Cliff. His short snout and weeping eye; his tail curved and tucked between his back legs so far that the tip brushed against his tummy.

I can't wait to take some more. Hopefully ones where he looks well and happy. That poor dog must have so many terrible nightmares trapped in his head, and I'm determined to replace them with good dreams that are filled with food and balls and sticks and blankets. When he comes home with me – because he absolutely has to – it will be the first day of his new life, a better brilliant life.

And then I have an idea.

It might be silly considering I don't know if Mum will definitely let me keep Cliff and I may as well say *goodbye phone* if she finds out, but I'm going to do it anyway. I open PicRoll and log out of my account before I see any updated stories from my friends. At the top is the *Set up a new account* option and I hit it, bringing up the next screen with all the boxes to complete. I work through, saying that I'm thirteen and using my school email address this time rather than Mum and Dad's home one. I know it's this easy because most kids at school lie about their age. However, guilt at disobeying my parents and telling a lie squirms in my belly but my brain scurries through ideas and plans. This is going to be so cool. I have to do it.

I get to the bottom of the page and press *Submit*. The next screen takes a second to load and then *Congratulations!* appears at the top.

"Yes!" I say under my breath.

I read the rest of the page.

Welcome to your new PicRoll account, Cliff. Get started and tell the world your story.

I skip the tutorial videos and pages – I know how to use PicRoll – until I get to the *Update your story* page.

Here we go.

Cliff the Abandoned Dog has his own PicRoll account!

I scroll through the photos I took of Cliff yesterday, and find one that's perfect. One where his one good eye is wide open so you can see the brown iris looking up at me; one that shows his skin and bones sticking out, but doesn't show too much of the sores on his neck and body. I select it, picking the best filter that makes the orange-brown on his snout glisten like it has glitter sprinkled on it.

And then I pause beside the image, the cursor flashing, as I think of what to write. I close my eyes for a moment and put myself in Cliff's head, imagine the fear and the pain and panic he must have felt yesterday. And then I write.

> I'm Cliff. I can't tell you what breed of dog I am or how old I am because I don't know. But today someone left me in the middle of nowhere, tied up with a rope to a tree. The note left with me said I was sad and ugly.
>
> I have sores all over my body and I am very hungry.
>
> But then, someone else found me and rescued me. I was scared at first, but then I realized the person who found me was kind and gentle and wanted to help me. I get to see him again soon! I hope I can trust him because I have lots of horrible memories from what happened before and I want them to all go away and be replaced with fun and happy memories.
>
> I can't wait to see him!

I read over it a few times, correcting spelling mistakes and grammar as best I can, but also not wanting it to sound like me, more like a younger child. I'm pretty sure Cliff is only a young dog, a puppy even, and I want his PicRoll followers to find his voice cute and lovable, and Cliff deserves all the love. Then, I work through the list of subject and interest boxes. It's a way PicRoll users get to see the photos, videos and stories they might like, that interest them. I picked loads of things when I signed up with my legit account, but mainly I scroll to the football and pranks and dog stories – which is how I had this idea.

I finish, wondering if I'm doing the right thing, worried Mum is going to find out. But, with a buzz of confidence and excitement, I hit the final button that makes my story – Cliff's story – go live.

And there it is. I look at it and read it again, over and over, smiling. The story of Cliff the Abandoned Dog. The first day of the rest of his life has begun. And with Cliff in my life, I know I can start feeling better too.

10

I duck down so no one can see me in the back of Mum's silver car. Pointless because we're no longer in Whaleview. I shake my head at myself and sit straight again, eyeing Mum and Dad in the front. I still haven't messaged Kai or Ted about tonight, and have silenced my phone so I don't hear their messages come in. I've never done this before, never let down my friends in such a massive way. They're going to hate me. I should let them know I'm not coming, but I can't bring myself to message anyone and tell more lies.

Especially after setting up Cliff's PicRoll account without Mum and Dad knowing.

Mum sings along to "Wonderful World" by Sam Cooke – definitely the most-played song on her playlist – and I do my best not to listen to the lyrics. They make me sad. Mum loves the old tunes. Says her grandma used to play them all the time and it fills her with warm memories. I think Mum's grandma was the only one who treated Mum like a kid; her grandma looked after all Mum's brothers and sisters while Mum went to hang out with her friends for a bit.

Mum's such a strong person so maybe I should try to be more like her. Just say how I feel, be honest like I was in the kitchen the other day. Or better yet, get over whatever is wrong with me.

"You OK?" Dad asks me, glancing from the driver's seat as we wait at a red light.

I do feel OK, other than my achy body and all the guilt about Kai's party, but I probably shouldn't admit that in case Mum ever speaks to Kai's mum. But also, I don't want them to worry about me because that might mean they don't let Cliff come home. And it's Cliff I need.

"Matt?" Dad asks.

"Ah, yeah, bit better," I reply. "Thanks."

Mum turns down the music and swivels to face me. Short strands of brown and blonde hair are stuck to the oversized, triangular collar of her black work top; she didn't have time to change before we left to see Cliff.

"You do look better actually," she says, brown eyes thinned slightly and examining me from around the headrest. "Maybe that's finally the end of your big growth spurt."

I nod, but there's a sinking feeling in my gut.

"Good job. You can't keep missing football games

and training, and now school. What's next?" Mum adds.

Kai's birthday, Jungle Warfare *sessions, not handing in homework.*

I swallow and look out the window, chewing the inside of my cheek.

"Nearly there," Dad says, which makes Mum face front and turn up the music a little louder than before, the song "Cupid" now blaring out and overshadowing some of my discomfort.

A few minutes later, Dad indicates and we swing off the highway into the small parade of shops where Rosie's Beach Vet is. There are more people milling about today than yesterday – two kids in a maroon school uniform bickering with their mum as they enter a mini-mart, a man in high-vis leaving a cafe holding a coffee and brown paper bag, and a few people wandering to and from their cars.

My chest feels a little tight – probably excitement at seeing Cliff – and I open the car door and step out into the warm afternoon sun. The car bleeps as Dad locks it and we head into the vet, Dad holding the door open for me and Mum.

There's a short lady standing at the reception desk with a white chihuahua in her arms, talking to Sue and a nurse in a green-collared shirt who sits behind the counter. Sue glances past the lady and acknowledges us with a smile. "Be with you in two," she says before focusing on the lady again.

So we sit on the hard plastic chairs in a line, and I take in a few deep breaths, eyeing the familiar animal food packets, worming and tick treatments, medicated shampoos, and healthy organic snacks. I know them well. Now we're here, I can't wait to see Cliff, to show Mum how cute he is and how important it is I take him home. I need to compose myself.

When I feel I have control of my breathing, I glance over at Mum and find her already looking at me.

"What?" I ask, a wave of paranoia washing over me. "Is there something on my face?"

"No. Nothing, Matty. Just looking at you. You're growing up so fast I can't keep up." She smiles, one of her soft ones that doesn't show her bright white teeth.

I glance at Dad, who's sitting with his legs crossed at the ankles, scrolling through something on his phone.

I shrug.

Mum lifts a hand and strokes my cheek with her palm.

I look away again but give her a small smile.

"I love your smile and I'm glad it's back!"

For some reason I want to yell at her for saying that. I don't want to talk about me.

The lady with the chihuahua leaves, her baggy,

floral-patterned trousers flapping as she steps through the glass door. It closes behind her with a *shush* and her tiny footsteps clip away quickly. Sue finishes chatting with the young nurse and then stomps round the reception desk.

"Hello to the Brown family! How are you doing?"

She's looking at me, so I answer. "Yes, good, thanks."

"Mum's here today as well," she says. "Lovely to meet you." Mum and Sue shake hands, making Mum suddenly not look as strong and bossy. I think Sue might be Mum's match!

"How's Cliff?" I blurt.

"Why don't we go and see?" Sue smiles, those yellowing crooked teeth now familiar, and she leads the way. Her trousers rub together noisily. "He is one very good boy, you know, I'll say that. Very placid, very sweet and when he isn't sleeping, he's a hungry one!"

"He did eat all our cornflakes," Dad says, giving me an elbow nudge.

Sue laughs. "He's been wolfing down all the food we've given him and then waiting expectantly for more. Bless."

We pass the room Cliff was taken in when we brought him here yesterday, the door closed, and continue along the white hallway to another room right at the back.

"He's still a bit on the nervous side," Sue says, "pretty anxious and frightened, so best to keep your movements calm and voices low when you first go in so as not to startle him." She raises her chaotic, hairy eyebrows and nods to me to make sure I understand.

It's probably Mum she should be addressing.

"Yes, definitely," I answer.

"Right." Sue pushes open a white door with a square window in the top half and we enter a small kitchen area, turn right into a new, shorter hallway lined with shelves of folded towels and sheets and white bottles and pots, and finally through another white door. It's a room about half the size of my bedroom. There are mats and toys laid out in the middle of the floor and four large, black cages sitting on tables on either side, all empty except one.

"Shut the door, please," Sue says to Dad.

I hear the door click behind me, my eyes already on Cliff. He's peering out through the metal bars of a cage, one ear poking up, the other flat. Both his eyes are open today, though one only a little. The other is so huge and wide, like a black golf ball.

"His eye." It's the first thing that comes out of my mouth.

"Yes, a little infected still but it's already looking much better since we've been treating it," Sue says, approaching the cage and lifting the latch. "Easily treatable, especially with such a sweet little boy." She says the last bit in a baby voice as she reaches into the cage slowly with one hand and strokes Cliff on his head. "Come on then." She beckons me over.

I inhale deeply and step forward, over the mats and dog toys on the floor until I'm beside Sue.

"Talk to him," she encourages.

"Hey, little buddy," I say, my voice whispery and a bit croaky, but I daren't clear my throat for fear of scaring Cliff. "Hey there."

"You can come closer. Give him a pat. Just nice and slow."

I stand right in front of Cliff and watch as he parks his butt on the furry brown and white blanket lining the bottom of his cage. He shakes a little, back hunched, curved, bones sticking out like a dinosaur. He cocks his head to one side, his sticky-up ear wibbling with the movement.

"I think he recognizes your voice," Sue says. "Keep talking to him."

I open my mouth to speak but don't really know what to say. Cliff stares at me and my heart becomes nothing but mush. He looks so sweet, so much better than yesterday, yet still sad and tiny. So skinny. And now that the rope is gone I can see how raw his neck has been rubbed. But he smells so much better today: a mixture of dog smell like Fifi and shampoo, but with a whiff of hospital to it, and his matted fur is gone.

"Have you had a bath?" I ask him. "I bet that was nice. You smell lovely." I clear my throat silently, swallowing the croak, the lump. "I can't believe how different you look. Your eye is clean and your sores are getting better too." Cliff tilts his head to the other side. "And … and you like eating, huh? I bet. And I think you should eat all that you can, put some fat on those skinny legs so we can go home and run about in the yard together."

I hear a sniffle to my right and turn to see Mum wiping a tear from her eye, Dad's arm around her shoulder.

"He's so skinny," she whispers. "Poor boy." I turn away. Mum cries all the time when she's watching the soppy TV dramas that she loves so much, but these tears are different. She looks like a child younger than me right now.

Cliff's head is following my movements. I grin and slowly lift my hand, palm up, towards him, into his cage. His brown eyes flick down to it and then back up to my eyes. They glisten in the lights of the room.

"Are you hungry now? Maybe I can feed you. Would you like me to feed you some yummy treats?" Cliff bows his head and sniffs at my hand, his cold nose brushing against my skin. And then his tongue pokes out and licks at my palm. It tickles and I giggle. Cliff stops and lifts his head, staring at me again.

We lock eyes for a few seconds, neither of us moving, me barely breathing, and then, just once, Cliff wags his tail.

I take another cube of soft squidgy meat from the bowl and feed it to Cliff. He has no teeth on the right side of his mouth, which was why the cornflakes kept falling out when he tried to eat them yesterday, so I carefully place it on the left side. Sue hasn't told us why he has no teeth there and none of us have asked. I'm thinking she doesn't know exactly, or doesn't want me to know. The thought of what might have happened makes my stomach lurch.

After Cliff has finished chewing in his awkward way, slurping the meat back into his mouth when it slides away from his teeth and licking up any dropped morsels from my hand and the floor, his tongue lolls out the right side of his mouth as he pants. He watches me with his enormous eye and wags the tip of his tail occasionally. They're only tiny wags but each one is the best thing ever and I want to make it happen again and again. He's not as jumpy either, though every now and then when one of us moves too quickly he ducks his head and shakes.

"What breed is he?" Mum asks, her black uniform now covered in animal fur too.

We're all sitting on the floor on the mats surrounding Cliff, though he's sitting between my outstretched legs right up close to my body on a fleecy green blanket. He doesn't seem alarmed by our faces all staring at him. I can't believe it considering how petrified he seemed yesterday. I think the food is helping. He really is hungry.

"Melanie and I have guessed he's maybe dachshund with those short little legs. Foxy. Maybe even chihuahua. It's hard to tell exactly. But I'd say a mixture."

It's my turn to cock my head to one side. Maybe I'll look up some breeds later to compare to Cliff's photos. I tickle him between the top of his front legs as he licks his lips, expecting more food.

"What happened to his fur?" Mum asks. She's stroking Cliff's back, showing way more interest than I expected.

"Could be a number of things, an allergy or an infection from insects or bacteria. He scratched his fur right off. Probably kept outside and not treated properly."

Poor Cliff. He continues to pant, pink tongue dangling out the side, and he's looking me right in the eye.

"We can always do another blood test to see his exact breeds, if you're interested."

I shrug, not too bothered. I kind of like the mystery surrounding Cliff. He's cute and that's all that matters. Plus, I imagine a blood test would mean more money, and the issue of paying for his vet bills hasn't come up again. I'm too scared to mention it, especially now that Mum seems to be falling for Cliff too.

"How old do you think he is?" Dad asks, tickling Cliff behind his sticky-up ear with his index finger.

"Again, hard to tell, but I'd say between eighteen months and three years. He's a young dog, and I don't think he has much more growing to do."

"Only outwards," Mum says, tucking some loose hair behind her ear.

"Yes, lots of outward growth and then he can have a big belly like mine!" Sue pats her tummy and snort-laughs.

The sudden sound startles me – and Cliff – and he starts up his shaking again. He bows his head quickly, nose dropping to my lap and face resting against my arm. I continue tickling his chest with my fingertips, my heart tensing at the fear in Cliff's reaction.

"It's OK, buddy," I say. "No need to be afraid now you're with us."

"I suspect he'll be a jumpy little thing for a while

yet. Lots of trauma to get over." Sue makes a sad face and nods a few times.

"May I ask what's happening with tracking his owners?" Dad asks, and his question makes me hold my breath.

"As I promised, I've chatted with my friends at the council and pound and he'll stay here for now. The owners have until Wednesday to claim him."

"But that's doubtful, huh?" Mum says.

"I'd say, wouldn't you?" Sue smiles softly. "If his owners do come forward, I'm pretty sure there'll be an investigation into possible animal abuse. Have you all had a chat about adopting him?"

I'm tempted to peer at Mum, still not sure how she feels about Cliff coming home with us, but I don't. The thought that she'll say no has been stabbing at my brain the whole time we've been here and that pain is too much to think about right now. "We're still chatting," Dad says. The adults fall silent and I avoid looking at their faces, pretty sure they'll be communicating in expressions, like adults do.

Cliff lifts his head and presses his snout further forward, until his head is pressed up against my tummy. I lean my head down, my back arching uncomfortably, until my forehead rests against the top of Cliff's. I close my eyes.

"It's OK. I promised you it would get better," I say.

We stay like that for a few seconds, until I can feel Cliff's body stop quivering, and then I lift my head to look at him.

"Well, I hate to spoil things as I can see you two are already the best of friends, but I'm going to have to get back to work and start shutting shop for the day." Sue climbs to her feet and brushes off her white jacket. "Do you think you can lift Cliff back into his cage?" she asks me.

Cliff looks into my eyes and I see my reflection in his big wide one. I smile. "Wanna go back to your lovely furry blanket for a sleep, Cliff?" He tilts his head, one side then the other, and then pants again, his tongue flopping out the side. His breath is hot and pretty grotesque in my face. "Bad breath boy," I say and place my hand under his belly, my other one under his butt. Slow, calm, gentle, and then I lift him. He's so light and so bony, it's like lifting an empty cardboard box, and I press him lightly to my chest as I climb to my feet. It's as if I'm carrying a giant bubble.

Placing him in his cage, he circles once and then lies down on his blanket, side pressed against the back of his cage, and lets out a long sigh, eyes still fixed on my face. I lean in and kiss him on the nose.

"Bye, buddy. See you soon." I glance up at Sue. "May I take a photo of him?"

"Sure thing," she replies, tossing the dog toys into a basket in the corner.

I snap a few pictures with my phone, and then kiss Cliff once more.

"Night, Cliff," Sue says and pulls a thin, blue blanket over his cage to hide him from the world completely. Sadness overwhelms me and I want to grab Cliff out of the cage and put him back in my arms, but I follow Sue to the door where she switches a radio on low and dims the light. Mum walks beside me down the corridor, her hand pressed into my back.

I have so many things I want to say, so many wishes and hopes and demands I'd like to make, but none of them are forming on my tongue. We reach the reception where another vet and two nurses dressed in pale green are chatting.

"You two head out to the car," Dad says, talking to me and Mum. "I won't be a second." He gives Mum a quick smile and a wink, rubbing at his hairy cheek. Sue says goodbye to us, and we leave the reception and step out into the warm evening.

The traffic on the main road whooshes past – loud and constant rumbles that were blissfully absent inside. I hate that life is carrying on as normal out here.

I clench my fists as Mum unlocks the car with the key fob and I climb into the back seat, my chest squeezing and jaw tensing. Mum shuts the passenger door and plunges us back into silence.

"Have you … have you decided yet? Can we keep him?" I ask, words strangled and squeaky.

"Pardon, love?" Mum peers at me, pink nails a contrast against the black headrest.

"Cliff. Can we keep him?" I stare at her, annoyance building because I know she's going to say no.

Mum sighs. "Dad and I will discuss it further this evening, OK?" She swivels back to face the front and I know without seeing that she's fiddling with her plain gold wedding ring. It's the only sign that my mum's unsure of what to say. I feel a tear trickle down my cheek. I slap it away quickly before her all-seeing eyes notice, or before more tears build into the fountain pressing at the back of my eyes – a pressure that seems to be a permanent fixture.

I need Cliff at home. I need him. I swear it will make me happier and healthier.

Dad comes out a minute later, climbs in the car and starts up the engine.

"All sorted?" Mum asks quietly.

Dad nods. "All sorted."

"What's sorted?" I ask, hating the way they're being

secretive. I feel so irritated and annoyed by them, by all the mumbling and whispering. Parents think their secret code is invisible to kids.

Dad looks over his shoulder, eyes connecting with mine briefly before checking for cars through the back window. "Just some more paperwork about Cliff."

"More paperwork? What about him?"

"Just to do with us finding him."

And we drive away, the radio playing some old Motown tune. Mum sings along like everything's normal, like it was before. It's obvious to me now: there's no way she'll let me keep Cliff, not after all the stuff she's said about us never having a dog and how much work they are. Even though she looked so interested in the vet, it was all just an act.

I'm going to scream. But I can't let the emotion out. I whip my phone out of the pocket of my shorts, needing to take my mind off not knowing if I'll see Cliff ever again. My chest tightens painfully, and that sinking, breathless feeling ripples under my skin – as if a river made of all the worst feelings and thoughts in the world rages inside me. But I need to get myself under control before Mum and Dad notice. I stare, eyes fixed on the screen, fingers opening apps and hitting names.

And as my eyes focus, I realize what I'm reading.

My text messages.

Ted: Mate, where are you?

Ted: What's happening?

Ted: Are you OK?

Ted: Kai's seriously annoyed.

Ted: Can you text?

Ted: Is your phone not working again?

My belly whirls, mouth watering as nausea rises. I click on Kai's name.

Kai: Are you coming tonight? My mum is ready to pick you up if you can't get to the restaurant. Call me.

Kai: Where are you? At least text me and tell me if you're not coming.

Kai: Whatever. You're out of order.

I drop my phone to my lap and rub at my face. Maybe it's better that Kai doesn't want to be my friend. I'm not exactly a supportive best buddy, like Ted, like I used to be. People like Kai and Ted, people with *real* problems, don't need me ruining their lives.

I'm such a joke.

12

Dad stops me escaping to my room when we get in and makes me stay in the lounge and watch TV with him. The fan spins fast in the middle of the ceiling and takes the edge off the humid evening. Dinner is homemade pizza and Caesar salad, but I can barely get any down. Guilt is pushing upwards from my gut, killing any hunger at all.

Guilt at disappointing my mates.

Guilt at lying to Mum and Dad.

Guilt that I've let down Cliff.

And then there's the anger.

Mum and Dad still haven't discussed if we can adopt Cliff, and I'm so furious with them for giving me even the slightest bit of hope. I knew it, I totally knew, but still I let the hope push through. But whatever Mum says, we do, and in this case it means Cliff might have to go to the pound.

All I want to do is shout and have a major tantrum like I'm five, tell her exactly how mean she is, how mean the world is.

I don't want to be here.

I frown at that thought, forehead crinkling, and glance over at Dad to see if he's noticed. Thankfully not.

He's sitting beside me on the leather two-seater and we're watching a repeat of an old football match – not that I'm really following the game right now. My heavy head's resting in my hand, but my wrist is starting to ache. I let my arms and head flop onto the squishy armrest of the chair, the leather creaking under my weight. All the emotion has wiped me out.

"Anything I can do for you, son?" Dad asks, patting me on the leg.

I let out a sigh and shake my head, drained of all my words.

Plates clatter in the kitchen where Mum tidies away. Dad cooked tonight – he definitely makes the best pizzas – so it's her turn to tidy up. I wasn't asked to help by either of them, and I'm definitely grateful for that. Just wish I'd eaten more so Dad didn't waste his time adding toppings that only I like. The animated chatter of the football commentators bounces around the room, and I hear the words they say, sense their excitement, but my head is stuffed with everything and nothing. I recall the text messages from Kai and Ted, over and over again, and run through different replies I could've sent   and still could, but don't. No matter what I think up, every excuse, it all sounds rubbish.

Sorry, wasn't feeling great.

Gutted I missed it but was sick again.

Can't believe I missed it. Hope it was fun.

My cheeks burn hot.

Mum wanders into the room and puts a steaming mug, the one I hand-painted for her for Mother's Day when I was at nursery, onto the small white table in the centre of the room. She kicks off her red furry slippers and collapses back on the armchair with an exaggerated grunt. I wish she wouldn't do that, and I openly eye roll even though it makes my head hurt.

"Who's winning?" she asks.

I don't bother to answer as I don't want to talk football with her.

"City. It's an old game though," Dad replies, after waiting a beat for me to respond first.

"Manchester?"

I do another eye roll.

"Yes, Manchester City," Dad says.

"Ah, yeah, great team."

I close my eyes, tears shoving desperately behind the lids, and wonder why I'm so irritated by everything Mum says today. She's not a bad person; she doesn't deserve me being so cranky with her.

A few more minutes pass in silence, me trying to

calm my annoyance, and I wonder about getting up and heading to bed. It's only a few minutes past seven, according to the silver clock on the wall where every number is a photo of me growing up, but my body is exhausted. And I definitely don't want to keep holding back tears; the pressure is giving me a major head and face ache.

Dad clears his throat and pats me on the thigh again. I open my eyes and peer at him. "Son," he says, "Mum and I have been chatting about Cliff."

I stiffen, holding my breath. "OK," I answer, drawing out the word.

"And, well, I've spoken with the letting agent and with the vet again – that's what I was doing just before we left earlier – and we've all agreed Cliff can come and live with us."

I lift my head. "Seriously?"

"Seriously."

"But how could we afford the vet bills?" I ask, looking between them both.

"Don't worry about that. We can manage it," Dad replies.

"But what if his owners change their mind?"

"We're not expecting that to happen."

Before I can let out any of the relief, of the gratitude swimming to the surface, Mum speaks in a sharp voice.

"But…"

There's always a "but" with her.

"But," she repeats, "it's a trial, Matty. We don't know if he'll want to live here; we don't know if we can give him the time he deserves – because he sure does deserve it." Her face drops slightly, eyes flicking down to the mug now in her hands. "And, you need to make us some promises."

I blink once, twice, waiting for her to continue.

"Maybe not now, hey?" Dad says.

I eye Dad who's frowning, in a begging kind of way, at Mum, but she shakes her head.

"No, Bri, it's important." She looks back at me. "Bringing this dog home is a big deal."

As if I don't know this already.

"And you need to show us that you deserve this. I need to see a lot more from you – at school, at home, at football. You need to make more effort with everything. Do you understand?"

I nod.

"You're almost a teenager and your body is exhausted from growing – I've been researching it – which means all the sleeping and the headaches are totally normal, but it's not an excuse to keep missing school."

"Yes, OK. I promise I'll try harder." These are the words she wants to hear, I know that, but I also do mean it. I believe Cliff is going to make me feel so much better, so I can be just like I was last year and the years before that.

Dad pats me again on the leg. "And Matthew, it's also OK to talk to me. You can always talk to us if you need to, about anything. We're here to support you."

"I think he knows that."

Dad doesn't acknowledge what Mum says, just fixes me with a stare. His brown eyes delve deep into my soul and I squirm on the inside, doing my utmost to keep the outside still and calm. I love Dad, and Mum, but talk to them? About all this, my weird crying and chest tightening, how I feel scared all the time? I don't know. I don't think I could ever tell them about all this stuff happening. How do you tell the people who love you most, the ones who give you everything and want you to be happy, that actually you aren't happy but you don't know why?

And anyway, it has to be linked to growing pains. Like Mum said. And when Cliff comes home I'll be better.

I nod and smile in response.

"I know, and thanks. Everything's OK." Hopefully it's enough for us to stop talking about this.

Dad keeps staring, as if he can see the lies and doubt in my head. I squirm some more, digging my fingernails into the leather chair, spinning my friendship band with the other hand, and look over at Mum.

"Thanks, Mum. I promise I won't let you down and I swear everything will go back to normal." I give her the most sincere expression I can muster and hope she believes me – Dad's better at sniffing out these kinds of lies than Mum. She's always too busy to spend much time on one subject.

She smiles back, her teeth flashing in the light of the wicker table lamp. "Love you, Matty. Let's see more of that beautiful smile of yours." She then turns her attention to the phone in her hand.

I don't look at Dad again; I can't, because for some reason, despite this brilliant piece of news about Cliff coming home to live with us, with me, I'm about to cry. I stretch, keeping it at bay, reaching my arms above my head and hearing my shoulders and elbows crack and creak. Ouch.

"I might go to bed if that's OK." My voice catches so I cough to clear it, hoping that it doesn't look forced and fake.

"You don't want to finish watching the match?" Dad asks, linking his fingers in his lap, eyebrows dipped in the middle.

Ugh, *guilt, guilt, guilt*.

"I do, but I want to be much better for when Cliff comes – and for school."

Guilt.

Mum folds her legs, tucking her feet under her bum. "Stay off that phone, please. Staring at screens all day every day isn't healthy at your age."

I stand, more guilt attacking, straightening gradually because my back feels stiff.

"Backache as well?" Dad asks.

I shuffle towards the hallway. "A bit."

"You should take the day off tomorrow, if you're still like this in the morning," Dad says.

"Day off for a backache?" Mum asks, her forehead wrinkled.

"Have you ever had a backache, Nat?" Dad asks her. She raises her eyebrows at him and shakes her head. I think Dad may have won that one. He looks at me again. "It's best to be completely better so get some more rest, yeah, and maybe take some pain relief?"

His words are like a fairy has granted my biggest, greatest wish, and I'm pretty much ready to collapse into a heap on the soft beige carpet and cry out my relief, my thanks. But I keep walking, nodding. "OK, probably a good idea."

I start climbing the stairs, bare feet sinking into the carpet. "Thanks," I call back. "Thanks for letting Cliff come to live here too." The first tear falls and my breath shudders, but I force it to remain silent so neither Mum nor Dad become concerned.

"You're welcome," Mum replies. "There's pain relief in the bathroom cabinet. Only take one pill."

"Will do," I choke out and then move as fast as my aching legs will carry me up the two flights of stairs to my bedroom, yanking on the handrail to help.

I click my door shut quietly and then crawl under my covers, not even bothering to change my clothes, to take the pain relief or brush my teeth or switch on the fan. Cliff's coming to live with me and I'm so grateful to my parents, so thrilled that I get to keep my promise to Cliff and show him not all humans are bad people, but all my body and brain want to do is cry.

13

I drag my body up my bed, rest my pillow against the wall and lean back. It's 9.30 a.m. I type the pass code into my phone and swipe away all the notifications quickly, before I can read them, other than the one from Dad telling me to check my bedside table. Before I do that I open PicRoll.

Cool air and singing birds and distant traffic sounds float in through my open window. My eyes are puffy and sting a bit this morning, probably from both the crying and the deep sleeping, but I do feel a lot better. Still achy and I have a bit of a headache, but I actually want to eat. My stomach grumbles loudly as I think about heading down into the kitchen to make peanut butter on toast.

I'm definitely getting better!

Once I've got some food, I plan to read through the pile of leaflets and booklets sitting on my bedside table about bringing home a new dog. There's a neatly written note paper-clipped to the top one from Dad.

Hope you slept well. I'm working two streets away this morning so call if there's a problem. I'll be home by midday anyway and Jane's next door too. She knows you're home alone. Rest up and feel better. Dad.

I smile. I look back at my phone and check the photo I added to Cliff's story. I plan to get the next one uploaded today.

My eyebrows rise as I see the number of smiley faces the PicRoll post has received.

Wow. 423. That's … surprising. I've never had that many on any of my posts before, not my *Jungle Warfare* uploads or my football reposts, not ever.

And the best part is there are twenty comments as well!

Excitement races through me, making my hands tremble as I open each comment bubble.

You are so not ugly or sad. Gorgeous boy.

Awww Cliff! You're the best. Happy new life!

Cliff you are THE cutest. I'm sorry that's happened to you!

Cliff!!!!! I love your sweet little face and want to give you a huge big fat kiss!!!!! You are gorgeous and I reckon you're about to have the best life from this day onwards!

That person loved exclamation points.

Sending you love, Cliff!

There are a few more like that, saying how cute and how lucky he is to have been found by someone so loving and special. I can't fight the smile, knowing that's me and that now I get to continue being loving and special for Cliff.

I scroll down to the last comment bubble and read.

Cliff, I hope your new family help you heal. It will be hard and you will have good days and bad days, but as long as you are always moving forward and making it to the end of every day, you should be proud of yourself. Here's to a wonderful future.

I read it again and then lay my head back, thinking about the words.

Good days and bad days.

Always moving forward.

I hope Cliff has more good days than bad ones, but I'm going to make sure we get to the end of every day and look forward to the next one no matter how hard it is. I swear I will give Cliff such a happy life.

Hitting the *Continue your story* button, I find the next photo to add. I choose the best one of Cliff in his cage at the vet, his one big golf-ball eye and one thin eye focused on the camera as he settled down for a good night's sleep. I sigh as I think of how comfy he looked cuddled up in the blanket; how his tail wagged as I fed him and his head tilted as he listened to me speak.

I upload it and choose a darker filter to show it's bedtime, and then I remember all the things Sue told me yesterday and type.

Here I am, in my special new bed. It was a scary day but I was looked after by some fantastic vets. So many things have happened. It hurt a bit having my fur trimmed and sore patches treated with special medicine creams. Look at my eye! Yesterday I couldn't even open it but now it's getting better. The world looks better through two eyes.

There's nothing wrong with my ear, it's just flat on my head all the time. I have lost most of my teeth on one side of my mouth but it doesn't stop me enjoying and gobbling up food.

And then the best thing happened!

The boy who found me came back to see me! I was frightened to start with but by the end was so happy and I even wagged my tail to show him.

119

I think it went well too because I've just found out I'm allowed to go and stay in his house one day soon. How cool is that? I have a new family that are going to love me and give me all those good memories I want.

Thanks for all of your comments on my first post.

I check it through and correct all the spelling mistakes and then hit *PICROLL*. I reply with a *THANKS!* to all the comments on the first post before putting my phone back down on the bedside table, deciding I'm not ready to look at any other notifications. Just the thought of my friends, of seeing photos of Kai's dinner, of reading the words that prove how upset they all are with me, gives me a rush of shame and guilt.

But I've decided: no more crying. No more. It's embarrassing and I need to stop being so miserable. Like Mum says: mind over matter.

I swap my phone for the pile of leaflets and start looking through them. There's lots of information that seems pretty obvious and things I think I'd do anyway – like giving your dog lots of space to adapt to their new surroundings, carrying on with your usual daily activities so the dog can get used to what's normal as quickly as possible, and setting a firm routine for play time, walks and dinner.

The next leaflet in the pile says: *Anxiety in Dogs.* I raise my eyebrows. I had no idea dogs could have actual anxiety about anything. I mean, I knew they could feel afraid, angry and excited, but not properly anxious. The first page lists behaviours to look for in anxious dogs:

Trembling

Tail tucking

Hiding

Panting

Pacing

Excessive barking

Diarrhoea.

Ugh, gross. There are a few more behaviours on the list, and I've definitely seen Cliff doing the first three. I carry on reading, learning about what can cause this anxiety – noting *abandonment* and *neglect* – and learning how to deal with dogs like this – ways to encourage him to relax and ideas for distracting and redirecting his attention when he's afraid. It's a lot to take in.

I put that one at the back of the pile and read the next title: *Depression in Dogs.* My frown returns and deepens as I read it again. Depression? Dogs can get anxiety *and* depression? My tummy does this unpleasant twisting thing that makes my legs shift under the blanket. I'm not sure I want to, but I unfold the leaflet and read. I scan through until I get to the *Signs your dog has depression* section:

Losing interest in play

Loss of appetite

Sleeping all day

Short temper

Hiding

Not getting up to greet you.

I swallow and fold the leaflet closed without reading any more, tucking it at the bottom of the pile and shoving them all on my bedside table. A weird ball has formed in my chest, and I chew the sore patch on the inside of my cheek.

My phone bleeps. A text. I glance sideways and see the alert light up. It's from Mum, and I let out a sigh of relief.

> Hope you're OK today, sweetie. You looked so peaceful this morning when I left so I didn't disturb you. See Jane if there's a problem. Dad will be home by lunchtime. Love you.

I text back.

> Much better, thanks. Love you too.

Yaps come from outside my window. I sit up and lift the corner of my blind. Sure enough, Fifi's out there charging about next door. I can't stop thinking about Cliff having anxiety and … depression, and I decide Jane might be the best person to talk to. I'm pretty sure Fifi came from the pound.

I heave my body out from under my blanket, leaving my phone on my bedside table with the leaflets, and change into a pair of plain black sports shorts and one of my Real Madrid jerseys. I'm slightly dizzy and a bit wobbly on my legs but I feel OK. I then head downstairs into the kitchen. I'm not as hungry as I was, but I make myself a chocolate milkshake because I know I need something in my belly. I wipe down the counter and put my glass and spoon in the dishwasher. No way do I plan on getting on the wrong side of Mum considering she'll be watching me even more closely from now on. I want to make sure everything goes perfectly with Cliff so she can see how responsible I am – and that I can be happy again.

I open the back door, the warm air caressing the skin on my cheeks and neck. It's a hot one and I hope we get some rain soon. The grass has turned a shade of light brown and is dry in places, and if anyone needs rain for their yard it's Jane. Stepping outside onto the decking, the dark wood warm on the soles of my bare feet, I listen and look for Jane and Fifi next door. They're there. Jane's voice hums along to music coming from her patio radio – she has one of those old-fashioned ones with the big dials on either side. She loves classical music, once telling me a few names of composers, some sounding a lot like famous football players.

I wander down the yard, peering over the wooden boundary fence. I see Jane crouched down, knees on her floral gardening mat, hands digging at the opposite border. She's wearing her giant sunhat with flowers all around the rim. It looks more like a fancy umbrella than a hat. Fifi spots me immediately and charges over with a happy yap.

"Hey, Fifi!" I say, squatting and stroking her little head through two white fence panels, the wood scratching my wrist. Fifi licks my hand and forearm and I giggle at how it tickles. "Good girl, Fifi," I tell her. "Good girl. I have a surprise coming for you soon."

I wonder how Fifi will act around Cliff, a worry worm wiggling in my belly. I hope she doesn't scare him, what with his anxiety and all. She's an excitable thing.

"Matt, hello. I didn't see you there." Jane plods across her small lawn to where I stroke Fifi, and I straighten. She has some dirt smeared across her green shorts.

"Hi, Jane."

"You look better today! I was sad to miss you when I came over for dinner on Sunday," she says, removing her gardening gloves and studying me. "But nice to see a bit of colour in those cheeks and a sparkle in your eyes."

I swallow, uncomfortable under her scrutiny. She has that same effect on me as Dad and Ted sometimes. "Yes, much better today. Thanks."

"Now, tell me. I heard that you're getting a dog. Clive. Is that right?" She grins, the already wrinkled skin on her face growing more wrinkles, especially around her eyes.

"Cliff," I say.

"Cliff, that's right. Of course, after your lovely grandad. Aww, so sweet. I can't wait to meet him. Your dad says he's had a rotten start in life." Her face creases up into a sympathetic expression.

"We think so. He was in pretty bad condition when we found him." The memory is enough to flip my stomach over.

"Well, isn't he lucky to have found you!"

I shrug. "I guess. I mean, it could have been anyone that found him," I reply, remembering what Mum said when we first told her.

"Maybe, maybe." Jane bends and scoops up Fifi, who licks at her face and neck. "But it was *you* who found him, Matt. You and your father, so I say Cliff is one lucky dog to have such kind and gentle people care for him."

I smile and nod.

"Fifi came from the pound, you know."

I look at Fifi's small furry face. "Yeah, I remember."

"Her first family didn't want her, though she had been well cared for and loved so her situation was nothing like what Cliff's been through."

No, probably not.

"Want some mandarin juice and lemonade?" Jane asks. "I have some mixed up in the jug."

"I, erm…" I glance back at my house, suddenly feeling the need to be back inside, but no. I have questions to ask. "OK, thanks."

"Great. Here, take Fifi." She thrusts Fifi over the fence and into my arms and then trots off down the yard to her patio.

Fifi continues her licking, but this time on my face and neck, and I snuzzle her back. "Wanna run around my yard?" I ask and place her gently on the grass at my feet. She sets off, sniffing as if she's the greatest dog explorer ever, on the trail to find the world's most valuable sticks to chew. She's so cute and watching her waddle about gives me excitement shivers. I'll be doing this with Cliff soon.

"Here you go." I turn as Jane passes over a tall tumbler of fizzing juice, ice cubes clinking against the glass sides. It's cold and wet in my hand and I take a gulp.

"Lovely, thank you," I reply, remembering my manners.

"You're most welcome, young man," Jane replies. "So, you're ready to look after a dog, are you?"

I nod. "Definitely. It's what I've always wanted." I've never been surer of anything.

"They are wonderful, but you have to be prepared to be patient and persistent."

I nod again. "I've been reading through a few leaflets about dogs. I have some good ideas already."

Jane rolls her glass of juice across her forehead, eyes closed. "Well, if you have any questions, you can always ask me."

I chew the inside of my cheek.

"I imagine the poor dog has some emotional issues," she adds.

I look at Jane as she gulps her drink, wondering if she's seen the leaflets already. "Do you think dogs can have … emotional problems then, like anxiety … and that?" I sip my drink.

"Oh for sure," she answers. "It's not just humans who feel things like that. My family used to foster dogs when I was a wee girl and lived in Troon, in Scotland, and I remember a lot of anxious doggy behaviour. From what your dad told me, it sounds like Cliff's showing plenty of that."

I swallow loudly.

"Which is really no surprise."

I don't move the glass away from my lips, pretending to still be drinking, willing her to go on.

"Thankfully it's easier to recognize things like anxiety and depression in dogs."

I swallow again. "What do you mean?" I ask, my quiet voice squishing around the sides of my glass.

Jane thrusts out a hip, taking her weight on one leg. "Well, dogs are happy creatures generally, needing food, water, exercise and love. And if they don't get one or more of those things they can become bored and even sad. Give those things back to a dog and they'll trust again and become happy – which you'll do for Cliff." Jane smiles, her eyes thinning kindly. "But us humans? Well, we're much more complex, aren't we? We don't always need an obvious reason to feel sad. Sometimes we just do."

I take in a deep breath, my eyes following Fifi as she snorts and snuffles around the fenced perimeter of my yard.

Jane leans against the fence. "Take me. I was ever

so low when my beloved John passed." She lifts her gold necklace and silently kisses the round, engraved pendant. "And after thirty-nine years with someone by your side, it makes sense to have a wee bit of the depression when they're suddenly not there." Silence lingers for a moment, both of us watching Fifi lower her butt and pee, before scraping her back paws across the grass to cover it up and kicking up a cloud of dust. Jane sighs. "But, my older brother, Kenny, poor lad suffered with depression all his life. I remember my parents taking him to see someone once. It was different back then; people didn't really talk much about it."

I nod, pretending to understand, and gulp down the last of my juice. I then pour the last of the melting ice cubes into my mouth and suck on them.

"I remember talking to Kenny quite a bit as he got older," Jane continues, "by phone, of course, because he never left Troon, and he would always say that he never understood why he felt so depressed, and when he couldn't find a reason for it that just made him feel worse." She rubs the pendant between her forefinger and thumb, blue eyes thoughtful. "But we were a close family, even though there were so many of us, and we all made sure to look out for him, right up until his last days."

I glance up at her, at her sparkly eyes and wrinkles.

"Talking to people helped me, and Kenny, but it was always good days and bad days. Here..." Jane takes my empty glass and I think about her words. *Good days and bad days.*

"We shouldn't be afraid of depression, however, and luckily with dogs it's easier to help them get better and I know you will do the most wonderful job, Matty. You will be his family now, you and your mum and dad."

I scrunch my bare toes into the grass, hoping she's right. I had no idea about all of this, but I am so ready to help Cliff get better.

Our two glasses chink together as Jane transfers them into one hand. "Right, Fifi, come!" And Fifi does exactly that, trotting over and wagging her bushy peacock tail all the way to where I stand. I scoop her up, kiss her snout and then help to wedge her under Jane's arm.

"Any questions, Matty, you know where I am, OK? Anything."

I nod. "Yes, thanks. I appreciate that."

"Back to work for me. These flowers don't plant themselves." She deposits Fifi to the ground and turns away, mumbling. "And these weeds certainly don't pull themselves out of the dirt."

Her classical music fills the void she leaves and washes away the strange sensation in my chest.

14

The odd car whips past me as I amble along the path to school, each time throwing up enough of a breeze to take the edge off the hot morning. Dad offered to drive me but I wanted to walk. I want to show him that I'm better, considering today's the day. I hold my phone up, writing the next PicRoll post for Cliff's story.

Thank goodness I *am* feeling better, because hopefully that means all my embarrassing behaviour is over too. No more weird breathing or feeling light-headed, no more forgetting everything, no more letting all the people down. And no more crying.

Good days and bad days. And my bad days are behind me. They need to be if I plan to look after a dog and prove how responsible I am.

Our visit to see Cliff last night was even more magical than on Monday. Mum came again and even fed Cliff a little bit this time, though she did wipe her fingers on a wet wipe after each time. We did pretty much all the same things and got lots more tips from

Sue about how to keep Cliff calm and relaxed, how to set up his bed and belongings in the house, and how to manage his sores and medicine. He's looking much better and thankfully his old owners are nowhere to be seen.

I'm so ready to bring him home.

I need to get this right, so that we get to keep him forever and ever. Dad spent a while with Sue filling out more paperwork and talking again; it seems to be nothing but paperwork, but I'm not complaining. Or asking any questions about how we're affording it all. I don't want Mum to change her mind and I don't care about paperwork if it means we're officially his new family.

And Cliff's past two PicRoll posts have gone wild. Last time I looked, his first one had 790 likes and over forty new comments. But his second, the one of him in his cage, had 2,563 hearts and over one hundred comments. I'm seriously blown away! Two posts and Cliff has so much support. There's no way I have time now to thank everyone but I have read through most of the comments.

People, complete strangers, have been reaching out to show their love and support for Cliff. Wishing him luck and good fortune from all around the world. A few comments are people sharing stories, about how they rescued their dogs from the pound. And some even shared their own personal stories of starting again, of being in a bad place and feeling frightened, but because strangers reached out to them, they were able to start over, new lives on new paths.

Each comment I read, my heart swelled and made me want to cry. Their stories were sad, but also filled with hope. Just like Cliff's new life. Filled with hope. That's what he needs.

I've already uploaded another photo of Cliff, one taken immediately after he chomped on a piece of meat, both his eyes huge and round as he waited for more, his ear pointy and perfect, and his tongue lolling out the side of his mouth. It's more of a close-up of his face than the others, and I know people following Cliff's story are going to love this one the most.

I'm early, already halfway to school, so I perch on a bench beside the road, thoughts of Cliff and everything Jane told me yesterday swirling in my brain.

I'm so happy today. My wonderful new friend has been feeding me so much delicious food. I have never felt so lucky. I have more energy too. But, some sad news, I did find out that I am suffering with anxiety and depression. I didn't even know dogs like me could be anxious and depressed.

It's going to take time for me to trust humans again, but all I need is more food and lots of love and then I think it will get better. I'm better already!

And guess what? Tomorrow's the day I get to go to my new home! The vet says I'm well enough and they're happy with my new family and the place I will live. It has a yard and another dog lives next door. I hope one day I am confident enough to play with her.

Anyway, stay tuned. I can't wait to share photos of the next steps in my new life!

Thanks for all of your love.

I check through as usual, wondering if I'm sharing too much – that someone will read it and know it's me – but all the words feel right and the support from strangers commenting on Cliff's other photos spurs me on. I can't believe people are so honest about their problems. And I didn't realize anxiety and depression were so common. I feel a bit silly really, but I'm also pleased I get to be the one to nurse Cliff back to health, and be one of those kind strangers I read about.

But first, I have to face school – and my friends.

I hit *PICROLL* and shove my phone in my pocket. My stomach's been in knots all morning – as I showered, dressed, left the house – every time I imagined Ted and Kai's reactions when they see me. I am sorry for not making Kai's party, because I know it would have been awesome, and I hope the *Jungle Warfare* voucher I bought him for his birthday helps.

My phone vibrates in my pocket. I sigh and pull it out again. It's a new message from Ted. Seeing his name sends my heart rocketing, but I can't ignore it. I haven't responded to any of his messages since Sunday – and there have been quite a few.

Ted: Hope you're all right. Having a kickabout on the field in about five if you're coming into school today.

I let out a relieved sigh and reply.

Me: Cool. Be there in a bit.

I put my phone back in my pocket, wondering if I should ask if Kai's mad at me. But at least Ted still wants to be my friend. The sun hugs me, but for some reason knowing Ted doesn't hate me for all I've done opens up this big hole in my chest. He's such a good friend, despite how busy his life is at home, and I have definitely not been a good supportive friend to him.

Tears threaten but I blink them away quickly.

No more crying, Matt.

The voice I hear in my mind is Mum's, but it's right – she's right.

I can start being a supportive friend again now, now that my bad days are over. So I speed up, pushing my feelings into each heavy step, and turn left onto Massocks Road where my school is. Waves of kids in green hop out of cars and whizz past on bikes, and I spy Joseph and his crew. I trudge on, hefting my bag higher onto my shoulder, clenching my fists and staring at my leather shoes taking me closer to my friends.

Once I reach the main gates, I barrel through with everyone and swing a right towards the fields. With more space in this area for kids to spread out, I relax a bit, and realize my tensing has given me a neck ache.

I spy my friends straightaway: Ted's hair stands out next to Kai's long blond hair tied back in a ponytail. I calm myself and head over. *Here we go.*

"Hey, Matt."

I turn to the unexpected voice and can't help the frown when I see Joseph jogging towards me. My belly sinks. What does he want?

"Hey, Joseph," I say, forcing my voice to not give away my apprehension.

"You back at football tonight? Didn't see you yesterday." He stands beside me, hair slicked back as usual, his bright blue eyes flicking from my face to either side of him and over his shoulder.

"Next week, I think. Not been well this week with … something."

Joseph nods, continuing to check around us, as if he's looking for someone. I look too, paranoia creeping in that I'm about to get ambushed or pranked. I start walking towards my mates again, pretty sure if I can reach them, I'll be safe – or *safer* – but Joseph matches my strides, one hand patting at his hair and the other stuffed into his shorts' pocket.

I'm not sure why he hasn't run off and I now get the feeling he wants to say something else.

"So, training was OK?" I ask, eyes fixed on Ted and Kai.

"Yeah, usual," Joseph replies.

"Cool." Another silence follows. A few more strides and I'll be with Ted and Kai, who've stopped tackling each other and are watching me approach.

I glance sideways at Joseph at the same time as he looks up and spies my friends.

"You're good then?" he asks, reversing now, back-stepping away from me, two thumbs held up.

"Yeah, good." I think so anyway. I have no idea what Joseph is really asking.

"Cool. See ya." And he whips round and sprints off.

Ted and Kai stand next to me. "What did he want?" Ted asks, frowning at Joseph's retreating figure.

"No idea. Asked me if I was back at training tonight." I shrug.

Ted nods and kicks his toe into the dry earth. "Are you?"

"Probably next week." Though just thinking about playing football makes me feel sick.

I face Kai, who's not looking at me but still at Joseph, and I take a deep breath.

"Listen, Kai, I'm sorry about Monday. I've been feeling rubbish but I should've let you know I wasn't coming." I squat and dig through my bag on the floor, removing his birthday card and voucher. I hand them to him. "Got you these."

Kai takes them. "Cheers, mate. I was pretty annoyed about Monday, but I know you've been ill. It's all good." Kai's never one to hold a grudge.

"Open it then," Ted says.

I smile and watch Kai rip open the envelope and look at the voucher. He grins. "Nice. Cheers." We bump fists and that's it. Next thing I know we're having a kickabout and everything I've worried about the last couple of days has been blitzed into nothing but a memory.

Science sucks. Mr Martin is much less forgiving than Kai and called me out in front of the whole class for not completing my homework.

And my mood has plummeted.

All morning I was feeling good: all was well with my friends, I was getting ready to tell them about Cliff next break, I was happy Ms Grassop never mentioned my Maths homework, and excited that the time to pick up Cliff was approaching. But now? Well, now I'm angry. OK, I didn't do my homework, but it seems being off school sick is not a good enough excuse for some teachers. Apparently now we're in high school it's our responsibility to tell our teachers our homework will be late or whatever. "Heard of email, Mr Brown?" Mr Martin said.

Ugh.

I grit my teeth and press my pencil down hard onto the page in my book, where I'm supposed to be answering questions on climate change. The room is silent except for the odd cough, shuffle of paper and scratch of scribbling pens.

My punishment: stay in through lunch break to complete my homework. No chance in heck I'm doing that. He can forget it. My mind replays his humiliating words, where he used me as a lesson for everyone. "Being in Year Seven means you're growing up. Excuses like 'I wasn't well' are simply childish..." That's the part that makes my hand scrunch the page right now, makes the rage tears burn my eyes. Why did he have to mimic my voice like I was some five-year-old kid?

My pencil tip snaps – and so does my temper. But even though my heart is drumming ridiculously hard, I don't leave class. Exhaustion is taking hold of me again. Plus, part of my mind is warning me that I can't do anything to jeopardize Cliff coming home, and Mr Martin is definitely the type to make a total over-the-top fuss if someone misbehaves. So I wait. I watch the clock, watch Mr Martin sitting at his desk like some sort of lord, his round glasses teetering on the end of his punchable nose...

I shake my head and look down at my trembling hands. What is wrong with me? It's not like I don't already know Mr Martin is the worst teacher, who picks on everyone about anything and everything. I did know. So why am I reacting like this? I place my hands either side of my head and press my thumbs into my temples, gritting my teeth harder. I can't make parent consultations worse than they probably already will be.

Chill. Chill.

Ted nudges my arm with his elbow and I peer at him over my hand. "You OK?" he mouths, forehead properly wrinkled.

Not now, Ted.

I nod and look away quickly. I do not need Ted making things worse right now. I need to get myself under control.

The black-and-white clock on the wall above Mr Martin's desk says two minutes to lunch bell, and I'm determined to be ready to leave with everyone else before he can call me back. The thought of disobeying a teacher plays havoc in my belly – but it's not as if I haven't broken other rules lately. Seems to be part of the new me.

I slide my bag closer under my desk and lower one hand so I can slowly and silently unzip it. The seconds tick by. One minute. One thing at a time, keeping an eye on the teacher, I slide my stuff inside my bag and zip it up, hand on the strap ready to grab and run.

And the bell goes. Other kids scrape back their chairs and noise erupts as everyone stands and packs away. I'm up on my feet, bag on my shoulder, and losing myself in the crowd of kids heading to lunch.

"Where you going?" Ted calls after me. "Wait up."

I screw up my face at him and he balks, but I can't explain or I'll be caught. With my face pointed away from Mr Martin, I file past his desk and out the door, just as I hear him calling me back.

"Matthew Brown, come back here, please."

No chance, sir.

And I race straight outside.

15

I stay in the toilets as long as possible until it probably looks weird and then I leave, looking for Mr Martin like I'm checking for beasts in *Jungle Warfare*, the same way I check for players coming to tackle me on the football pitch. I need to make it down to the field without getting caught.

I have no idea what came over me back in Science, why I behaved that way and thought those terrible things about Mr Martin, but now I've cried it out of my system in the toilet cubicle I'm pretty ashamed. I wish I had some sunglasses to hide my red eyes, but hopefully splashing my face with cold water has helped.

Ted and Kai are set up in our usual spot under the vast, sweeping tree that creates enough shade for about five pockets of kids to sit and eat their lunch protected from the sun. I toss my bag down and sit with them, removing my lunch with hands that are still shaking. I don't say anything, just try to act normal.

"You OK?" Ted asks quietly.

I swallow and nod. "Yeah, why?" I don't know why I'm acting all tough like this, because inside I am definitely *not* feeling tough.

"Well, you were a bit weird back there in Science."

I glance at Kai, who's eyeing me as he picks chunks off his bread roll and puts them in his mouth.

"Was Mr Martin annoyed?" I ask, peeling my orange.

"'Course he was. Didn't you hear him calling you back?" Ted's already finished eating his lunch. "Mate, I've never seen you act like that before. Like, why didn't you just do your homework?"

"Was it the acid rain stuff?" Kai asks. He's not in our Science class.

"Yeah," I answer.

"That wasn't hard. I mean, even *I* found it easy." Kai lets out a snort-laugh.

I gulp down a segment of my orange. So why didn't I find it easy? Why didn't I do this *easy* Science worksheet when it was first set?

We fall into silence as we eat our lunches, but my appetite has disappeared, my gut full up with a nervous heaviness I've become so used to lately. I slide my lunchbox towards Ted. "Want anything to eat? I'm not hungry."

"You sure?" Ted says, peering in.

I nod and stand, stretching my arms above my head

and cracking my back. Only seventy more minutes left of school and it's Cliff time. I need today to be a good day. *Good days and bad days.* I'm not giving up yet. What problems do I really have to be annoyed about anyway? So a teacher is mad at me. At least I'm not Ted who has to do a ton of chores at home, including his family's grocery shopping every week as his mum works such long shifts. That thought reopens my sadness hole and I feel the tears again.

Nope. No tears.

I turn back to my friends and slide the ball out from behind Kai with my foot. I chip it up and kick it from one foot to the other as I move into some space in the scorching sunshine. The ball moves naturally between my feet, and I wonder why I've been so afraid to play this season. I guess that's all in the past now.

Good days and bad days, I suppose. Maybe I *can* go back to training next week.

Kai joins me and I tap the ball to him, ignoring the butterflies in my tummy launching into flight.

I grab my khaki camouflage wallet and charge out the front door. Dad locks up behind me. It's time!

"Hey, you two!" Jane is grabbing grocery bags out of the boot of her car and carrying them to her front door. I hop over and prise them from her fingers. "You are a dear," she says, plucking her door key from her bag knitted in the shape of a massive daisy.

"No problem," I say. "We're off to get Cliff." I don't know why I tell her, why I blurt it out like I'm some little kid. I guess since our chat yesterday I thought she'd want to know. She opens her door and, bringing a strong floral aroma with her, Fifi charges out, snuffling around our ankles and then leaping up on her back paws, tail wagging so fast I'm worried it might fly off.

I hope Cliff's tail wags like that one day.

"Oooh, how exciting, Matty," Jane says. "Pop the bags just in the hallway, lovie, would you?"

"We'll take them into the kitchen, Jane," Dad says behind me, and I turn to see him with four green reusable shopping bags weighing down his arms.

"Thank you, Brian. Strong like my John."

I've been in Jane's house loads of times before, when I was in primary school, though not this year and that makes me feel kind of sad. It has the same layout as ours. Fifi yaps around my legs and tries to climb into the shopping bags. I carry them through into Jane's kitchen, placing them on the square kitchen island. Dad comes up behind me and heaves the four bags he's carrying onto the island as well. There are plants everywhere in Jane's house – colourful flowers and greenery all over her window sills and in wooden pots and ceramic dishes on the kitchen counter and little round dining table. Jane has an outside and inside garden.

I know Mum and Dad would like to do more in our garden, and redecorate the house, but as we only rent, it's not ours to change. But one day, Mum always says. Life is expensive, and though they try to save for a house deposit, they still have to pay out a lot of money all the time on things like bills, food, cars, school excursions and uniforms … and my football club fees.

I chew the inside of my cheek as guilt chews the inside of my mind. Somehow they've already paid for Cliff's expensive vet bills and adoption fees, for me. And here I am without a care in the world expecting them to start paying for us to keep a dog permanently.

I press my hand against the wallet in my football shorts' pocket. I've got all my leftover Christmas money; I'll referee extra games at the club, and make sure I pay for as much as I can when it comes to Cliff.

"You have time for a cuppa?" Jane asks, filling up her cream kettle at the tap.

"That's kind of you, but we're headed to the pet store first to get some essentials for Cliff," Dad says, pulling the truck keys out of his jeans' pocket.

"Of course. Of course. Oooh, you must be so

excited, young man," she says to me.

"Yeah, I can't wait."

"What are you going to buy him?"

"Well, we need a bed for him and some blankets, a few toys and food, and maybe a brush and…"

Jane giggles, making me pause. "You're a good wee lad," she says, and I cringe. "Honestly, I think as long as that dog has you, he'll be happy."

I smile. I hope she's right.

"Right, come on, son," Dad says.

"I cannot wait to meet him." Jane follows us to the front door, Fifi too. "And I think Fifi feels the same way!"

I bend down and stroke Fifi, letting her lick my hand for a second before I step out the front door.

"Thanks for your help with the shopping. I don't know where I'd be without you three."

I glance up at Jane and wave goodbye. She shuts her front door and I climb into the passenger side of Dad's truck. Mum works late on Wednesdays, so it's just the two of us collecting Cliff.

Dad reverses off the drive and pulls out onto our quiet road to the roundabout at the end of the complex, out through the tall electric gates and onto the highway. We pass the national park where we found Cliff. That day feels like so long ago.

"How was school today?" Dad asks.

I look out the window, focusing on the passing shops and warehouses lining the busy road. "All right, thanks."

I turned round my bad mood in the end and managed to avoid Mr Martin for the rest of the day. Of course I'll have to deal with him Friday when we have Science again, and I'll definitely make sure I have the homework completed beforehand.

"Yeah? Nothing much going on then?"

"Nah, just usual school, you know."

"By the way, did you miss Kai's birthday? I put it on the calendar, but you never mentioned it again."

Ugh, I forgot. "Oh yeah, erm, it was Monday but I didn't feel well enough to go." I side-eye Dad at the same time he does me and our matching brown eyes lock. After a second he looks back to the road and I wait for him to say something.

"That's a shame," he says.

And then we fall back into silence, only the loud growling of the truck's engine and the clattering and banging of Dad's tools in the back to accompany us on our journey.

16

We step into the air-conditioned space of the vet's reception area, the glass door closing with a gentle *swoosh* behind us. An unfamiliar nurse in uniform greets us with a smile. "Hello, can I help?" she says, her voice warm and welcoming.

Everything is so calm in here, the busy road shut out behind us, but my heart feels like it's going to explode.

"We're here to collect Cliff," Dad answers, leaning his elbows on the speckled counter.

"Oh yes, we're expecting you, aren't we?" She shuffles around in a drawer beside her and removes some papers joined together with a yellow dog-shaped paperclip in the corner. "Right, let's look through the paperwork. So much of the stuff."

She laughs loudly as Dad says, "You're not wrong."

"Though, looks like you've done most of it already and we just need a signature or two so the adoption is official."

I'm overcome at hearing those words and bite too hard on the inside of my cheek, instantly regretting it as my mouth fills with the metallic taste of blood. I hug the blanket I just bought Cliff, grey with a black bone pattern, and it feels soft against the skin of my forearms. I focus on that feeling as I make myself chill out, and then I look back up at the nurse.

She's staring right at me with wide, penetrating eyes that are rimmed with thick black make-up.

"While Dad's signing all this, why don't we head back and get Cliff?" she says in a voice that suggests she thinks I'm younger than I am. But she's sweet so I bury my annoyance and nod.

"Yes, please."

She leads the way, rabbiting on about the weather being so hot for this time of year and that there's "bundles more traffic on the roads now" which makes her have to leave earlier for work. My breathing speeds up as I struggle to zone her out. I wish she'd stop talking because her voice is making my chest tight, and she sure speaks fast. We stride down the corridor, a meow followed by a whining dog emanating from behind white doors, punctuating the quiet of the place. We reach Cliff's room and the nurse, Aisha, pushes open the door.

I see him straightaway, peering out of his cage. He's

sitting, nose pressed against the bars, both eyes big and wide and wet-looking.

As I approach, he cowers, head dropping.

"Oh, Cliffy baby, look who's come to see you." Aisha lifts the clip on the lock and swings open the cage door. Cliff withdraws to the back, his head lowering even more, that horrible, heart-stabbing tremble back in his body. My stomach drops, scared he's forgotten me, that his little head is filled with all the bad stuff again.

Good days and bad days.

I put down the blanket and inch closer to him. "Hey, buddy. Hey, Cliff," I say, voice just above a whisper. "It's me. It's Matt. I'm here to take you home."

Cliff keeps pressing himself to the back of his cage, but I see his eyes flick once to mine.

"Keep talking. He'll come round," Aisha says beside me, and she starts humming along to the song playing on the radio.

So I do. And gradually, the more I speak, the more Cliff lifts his head and the more his eyes linger on mine each time.

"We had another dog in here today – a loud one that whined a lot – and I think it disturbed his quiet." Aisha giggles. "Maybe some food will coax him out. Not too much before a car journey, of course."

She hands me a small plastic tub of the meat cubes

we've fed Cliff on previous visits. I pluck one out and ever-so-slowly edge it towards Cliff. "Come on, buddy. You love this stuff. Remember? It's juicy and delicious and I know you want it." After a minute, tiny black nose twitching as he sniffs the cube, his snout moves closer and he opens his mouth to take it. I push it into the left side of his mouth to help him and he gobbles it up.

I release a breath and smile, letting Cliff lick my fingers with his rough, pink tongue. I take another piece of the meat with my other hand and feed him that too. I keep going until Cliff is looking at me, and I'm willing him to do that one wag at the tip of his tail.

"Pick him up when you're ready," Aisha says.

"Really?" I ask.

"Sure. I'm here to help you." She smiles, all cheesy, her brilliant white teeth bright against her skin. "Nice and slow but be firm at the same time."

I place a hand under his chest and the other under his bottom and lift him forward and then against my chest. Aisha feeds him a piece of meat as I rearrange my hands and hold him close. He's so warm and perfect and I just want to cry.

I'm holding *my* dog.

"Right, do you want to bring him out to reception? I reckon your dad will be finished with the boring stuff.

Now remember, he'll likely do a lot of sleeping for the first few days; he has a lot to recover from. But just go with it and don't be alarmed."

With Cliff in my arms, Aisha's voice and babyish talk doesn't bother me so much. I nod and she smiles again.

"Right. You take your blanket" – she drapes the bone blanket over my shoulder – "and I believe Sue said you can take the brown furry one he's been sleeping on too." She removes that one from the floor of his cage and opens the door. "Sue's out on visits this afternoon, but she's already said her goodbyes. She's left a pack of instructions and ointments, and she'll give you a call tomorrow to see how things are going. Off we go then, Cliffy baby. Off to your new home."

I hold Cliff nice and firm, one arm and hand hugging him to me, and stroke his head with the other hand. He presses his face into my chest and I kiss him on the head. His fur and bare skin patches are soft and cool. I lay my palm against his tiny face and whisper in his ear, "I love you."

Dad places the bag of biscuits, tray of tinned meat and bag of dog toys that we bought in the pet store at my feet and closes the passenger door of his truck with a gentle thud. I've laid the bone blanket under

Cliff, who sits on my lap, and covered him in the furry brown one. He's shaking so much, but I keep holding him tight and stroking and kissing his head. Dad hops in the driver's seat and we set off into the rush hour traffic.

Neither Dad nor I speak to each other, but I do see Dad glancing my way as I talk in a low, soft voice to Cliff all the way home. Cliff doesn't lift his head once, just keeps it flush with my chest. I don't really know what I'm saying most of the time, my head jumbled up with all kinds of worries and thoughts. Barely taking my eyes off Cliff, I sense Dad shutting down the engine and plunging us into silence. I look up; we're parked on our driveway. That was the fastest journey of my life.

"Right, ready?" Dad asks me, speaking softly.

I nod. Dad releases the button, and I manoeuvre my arms and Cliff around my seatbelt as it slides back. Dad opens the truck door for me, and I climb out and head towards the front door, which Dad also opens. I couldn't have done any of this without him.

I try to fight back a sudden wave of emotion as I step inside the house, bringing Cliff into my home for the first time, but tears tumble and spill anyway. I decide these aren't the silly sad tears that I've been crying so much lately, but happy ones, and so I let them fall. I sit on the sofa, Cliff still in my arms, and kiss and stroke him over and over. Dad doesn't say anything about my crying, but as he lays the bone blanket beside me, I notice how his eyes glisten in the setting sunshine pouring in through the glass lounge doors.

Carefully resting Cliff on the blanket, I lie beside him, head on the beige cushions, my arm still wrapped around his skinny body. Cliff's eyes are drooping closed and I run my palm across his head, flattened ear and his shoulders and tummy and bony back, avoiding his sore patches and smoothing his tufts of fur until they feel silky. The tears keep falling and I'm utterly powerless to stop them, and then Cliff licks them off my cheek. I close my eyes and smile.

"I will never ever let you down, Cliff. Never."

He stares into my eyes and I watch as his close. But I don't look away, not until I also drop off to sleep.

17

I hear the click of the front door as Mum comes in from work. I blink a few times until my eyes are ready to open properly and watch her kick off her black flip-flops and place them on the white wooden shoe rack at the bottom of the stairs. She then hooks her shiny red handbag over the stair rail and places a brown paper bag on the second stair. Dad greets her with a kiss and they share a few lowered words, and then she spots me. Her palms join as if she's praying, and she makes an O with her lips, head tilted to the side, which sends the ponytail on top of her head cascading to the side as well.

"Look at you two," she says in a sing-song voice, and tiptoes over.

My arms are dead but I daren't move them and disturb Cliff, though I know I'll have to soon. Dad eases back into the chair opposite, the one Mum usually curls up in every evening.

Mum crouches in front of me. "How did it go, the

pick up at the vet?" Her voice is gentle and I'm surprised as Mum doesn't do quiet. She's naturally loud.

I smile, not wanting to talk – partly too tired and partly because Cliff's breaths are calm and even, and he's snoring quietly. But thankfully Dad fills Mum in as she alternates between stroking Cliff's head and mine.

"I'm so pleased, Matty. So, so pleased." She lingers for a moment, looking at me, hand resting on my hair, as if she wants to say something. I smell her work: shampoo and conditioner and other hair products. Then she stands, grabs the paper bag from the hallway stairs and heads into the kitchen, all on silent bare feet. I've never known Mum to be so quiet.

I shift my eyes to the TV, to a fishing show – something Dad used to do with Grandad when he was a kid. The volume is low but Dad seems happy, reclining back in the chair, legs crossed at the ankles. A delicious, greasy smell drifts from the kitchen and I hear rustling and plates clinking as Mum potters about. Cliff opens his eyes and lifts his head a little, but doesn't move. Next thing, Mum's carrying in two white dinner plates, burritos and nachos piled high on each. She hands Dad one first and then turns to me.

"You'll need to sit up, my love," she says, placing the other plate down on the floor. "I'll take Cliff." She scoops him up before I get a chance to agree and I'm about to argue with her but pause, noting how gently she slides him away from me. She envelops him in her arms and covers him with the bone blanket. Then she bobs him up and down, cooing and whispering into his ear. And Cliff, well, he doesn't seem too bothered to be disturbed and he's staring right at her.

I sit up, lifting the plate of food onto my lap. Mum's been to Curly's Burrito Bar, my absolute favourite, and just like that I want to cry again. She's gone out of her way to make this a special day, through food like she often does, and I know this because we can't afford Curly's often.

I pick up my burrito and bring it to my lips. I bite into it, but I can't seem to chew or swallow because I'm utterly overwhelmed with emotion. Gratitude, sadness and guilt back again – probably because I've had so many bad thoughts about Mum lately. I hold the food in my mouth and rub at my eyes, hoping my parents think I'm just scrubbing the sleep away. It takes me a second to compose myself and catch my breath and then I eat, needing to show Mum I'm fine.

I'm not as hungry as I wish I was, but force down as much of the food as I can, all the time watching Mum wander between the rooms with Cliff in her arms, singing Marvin Gaye and Stevie Wonder songs to him softly.

Dad wipes his hands, stands and takes my plate and his to the kitchen. He washes his hands and both he and Mum re-enter the lounge together. The cushion sinks as Mum sits beside me.

I move closer and nuzzle Cliff, running my thumb between his closed eyes. He's not shaking and he feels warm and looks comfortable.

"He really is a cutie pie," Mum says, and she gives him a peck on his snout.

For someone who didn't ever want a dog, I can't believe how good she's being with him. But then I guess she raised a baby – me – and perhaps it's not much different.

She glances at the clock. "Wow, seven-thirty already. I'd rather Cliff didn't sleep upstairs so I think maybe we set him up a bed down here."

My jaw drops, but before I can say anything, Dad speaks first.

He leans his head and shoulder against the archway that joins the lounge to the dining area. "But, for tonight, you can sleep down here with him, OK?"

"Only for one night, though, right?" Mum adds, eyebrows raised.

"OK," I reply, too tired to get into a discussion about it now, especially when she's got that "I'm not open to negotiation" expression going on. I didn't think the tough Mum would be away for long.

"Right, so where should we set up his bed?" Dad asks, scratching his hairy chin.

I glance around the room, out into the hall and the kitchen-diner. There are white tiles everywhere, cold and hard, but soft carpet in the lounge. "I think in here. It'll be more comfortable and warmer."

Mum sighs and studies the beige carpet. She nods. "OK, but if he makes a mess, you clean it up straightaway. We can't be getting in trouble for a dog soiling the place."

"Yeah, no problem." Gross. I didn't think about that. But I'll do anything to show Mum I can be responsible, that she can rely on me.

"OK, well, I'll go get the supplies you bought out of the truck. Why don't you take Cliff in the yard for a wee and then we'll clean him up for bed?" Dad tilts his head in the direction of the back door and then grabs his keys from the hall table and goes out the front.

"Here you go." Mum removes the blanket from Cliff and holds him out to me. I stand and take him, and with his softness back in my arms we go through to the kitchen. Mum switches on the outside patio light, flooding the back garden in golden light, and opens the door for me.

I look at Cliff, his head now raised and eyes wide

and alert. "Ready to see the yard for the first time?" I ask him.

His watery, black eyes glitter as he looks at me, and I kiss him and step into the cool evening.

Fruit bats cry and swoop between trees and houses, impressive in the star-studded purple of the night sky. I breathe in the fresh air, filling my lungs, and wander across the decking. It creaks beneath us and I reach the end where I sit, feet on the grass. "Wanna go down on the ground?" I ask. He's looking about the yard, head darting from side to side, ducking as a bat beats its vast wings overhead. "Nothing to be afraid of, Cliff," I say, stroking him. I gently place him down, until his tiny paws touch the grass, and run my hand over his body.

"You're safe here," I tell him. "Safe."

Cliff quivers by my leg, continuing to check out the yard, his warm body in contact with my skin. His head reaches halfway up my shin and he looks so delicate beside the muscle of my calf. "It's OK," I say, "we'll walk together." And I get down on my hands and knees and I shuffle forward, again and again, Cliff inching forward with me. I move slowly, gradually, not wanting to scare or startle him, and then, suddenly, obviously desperate, he pees on the grass.

"Yes!" I whisper, a tiny celebratory shake of my fist. "Toilet visit successful."

I continue to perform a small circuit on my hands and knees, not venturing far from the deck, Cliff sniffing at the grass as he investigates beside me. The bright beam from the outside lamp casts Cliff in an angelic glow, and I decide I'm going to become his protector for as long as I possibly can.

Removing my phone from my pocket, I squat and snap a few pictures of Cliff as he wanders, never too far from my feet, nose twitching close to the ground. He stops occasionally, lifting his head and listening to the night sounds of the bats and distant cars. It's peaceful out here and I'd like to stay longer, but Cliff has plonked his butt down, head bowed forwards.

I bend down and pick him up, hugging him close. "Let's get back in, hey?"

In the lounge, Dad has laid the furry grey dog bed, far too big for Cliff, on the floor by the sofa, and Mum puts the final touches to the makeshift bed she's set up on the sofa for me.

"Right, son, why don't you head upstairs, have a wash and do your teeth, and I'll deal with Cliff's eye drops and sores," Dad suggests, and, though I'd like to be the one to do all that for Cliff, I'm nervous too. So I say OK and do as Dad says.

A few minutes later, back in the lounge, I sit on the orange cotton throw on the sofa. Mum kisses me and then gives Cliff a little peck. "Dad and I are heading up to bed now too. We're shattered. I hope you both sleep well."

"Bye, buddy," Dad says. He ruffles my hair once and tickles Cliff on his flat ear. "Get some sleep and come up and get me if you're worried – about anything." He puts emphasis on the last two words and I nod.

"Thanks, Dad. Mum. Thanks for letting Cliff come home. I won't let you down." The final words get caught in my throat.

Mum flicks on the lamp on the coffee table and grins. "Anything for you, my darling. You're my boy." She then bounds up the stairs. Dad, after locking the front door, follows her at a slower pace, giving me a wave just before he disappears.

I kneel on the floor and deposit Cliff onto his squishy bed, building up walls around him with the two blankets, and then I rustle in the bag from the pet store and remove the Winnie the Pooh cuddly toy I bought. I snuggle it beside him, and then I grab my pillow and the throw from the sofa and make up my bed next to him on the floor. Before settling, I take a few more photos of Cliff all curled up in a tiny ball in his blanket fort, telling him how cute he looks, and then I lie down.

I open PicRoll.

My eyes bulge at the 5,630 likes and 1,425 comments on Cliff's last post. Wow. People are loving Cliff the Abandoned Dog way more than I expected. I glance sideways at him and see him staring at me, chin resting on his paws, and I smile. "You're a superstar!" I whisper.

He sniffs, readjusts his back legs and then closes his eyes.

I choose a photo of Cliff outside in the yard, his tail curled under and between his back legs and upload it.

Well, here I am. In the backyard of my new home. The boy came to collect me from the vet and then his dad drove me to his lovely, warm house.

I HAVE A HOME!

The yard is quite big and scary, but my boy showed me how to walk on the grass, getting down on his hands and knees and pretending to be a dog. It was quite funny, but it helped. And then I took a pee and marked my scent. I sniffed the air and definitely smelled another dog nearby, as well as a whole load of other creatures.

I didn't stay outside too long because I got pretty scared of all the big bats and the dark sky. I have a lot of fur missing still but when it grows back I think I'll stay warmer. My boy took me inside and we had a big cuddle and I think I'm going to be pretty happy here!

Check out my new bed! My boy bought me all this cool stuff from the store, including this Winnie the Pooh toy, and it is all so soft and cuddly. I'm pretty tired after such a big day, but I hope when I wake up I'll be ready for so many more adventures. My boy is making me feel safe and brave, and I feel so lucky to have him as my friend. I didn't realize how much I needed someone to show me not to be afraid, to show me that I'm not that ugly and unwanted, and that life could be awesome.

AND I LOVE IT HERE ALREADY.

But there's something else...

I want to help my boy too, because I don't think he's very happy. I think he might have some problems he's too scared to talk about, all buried deep inside his tummy. I know what that feels like. But I'm here for him and maybe together we can get better.

18

Mum leaves early for work; I hear her banging around upstairs as she gets ready, and then I both hear *and* smell her making coffee in the kitchen. The mixed aroma of her perfume and the bitter coffee churns my stomach, but I don't react. I pretend to be asleep, my hand resting on Cliff's paw. I stayed up so late last night, staring at Cliff's tiny, delicate body in his bed, thinking so many weird thoughts. I'm so happy he's here, so, so happy, but after writing that last PicRoll post, it's as if I've opened a trapdoor in my chest and let a whole bunch of my emotions out.

I don't really know why I posted it, what made me do it. Cliff the Abandoned Dog is about Cliff starting his new life, his new *happy* life. Not about me and my … problems. What have I done? I should never have done it, never have made it about me. People will probably stop reading Cliff's posts now. Something else I've selfishly ruined.

I'm breathing out my mouth as my nose is completely

blocked, and I have a stinking headache as well. *Thump, thump, thump* it goes. I guess that's what comes of trying to keep your crying inside. I keep attempting to open my sore eyes to look at Cliff, but they're so heavy and the light flooding in through the lounge blinds is harsh and urgent and they just keep closing again.

But the worst part is the sick feeling in my tummy. My chest isn't tight; everything I feel is down in my stomach now. It's swishing like I'm on a horrible roller coaster that's doing loop-the-loops over and over and faster and faster. I want to vomit and scream and yell and squeeze my fists all at once, to stop this evil ride. I don't understand it, and I really, really don't like it. It's as if I've lost control of my insides and my brain isn't trying to help.

This is not a good start to having Cliff home.

In fact, it's an absolute disaster.

Like me.

I can't do this.

But I don't even really know what "this" is right now.

I thought having Cliff here would make me happy, and it does, but still some weird sadness is commanding my brain and body.

I lie still, letting fresh tears fall from my closed, crusty eyes, focusing on the soft fur of Cliff's paw pads beneath my fingers and palm. Everything feels so wrong, everything apart from Cliff. And the thoughts in my head are worse than wrong.

A while later I hear Dad in his and Mum's bedroom right above me, and I know when he makes it downstairs he'll be annoyed I'm not already up and dressed for school. But it's too hard to lift my head, my body, to even think my way through all the things I have to do to get ready. Let alone all the things I will have to do when I get to school. To be honest, I don't even know what day it is so how can I prepare for any lessons?

And how can I possibly tell Dad what's really wrong? I don't even know why or where this has all come from. I don't get it, I don't want it.

I let out a sob that comes from deep in my gut and let the tears cascade down my cheeks, that river of emotion seeping from the inside out. I was supposed to show Cliff that life was good; I was supposed to be the one to save him. Yet here I am, the one who clearly needs to be saved.

I'm embarrassed and ashamed and filled with the worst guilt I've ever felt in my life.

I'm a failure. And I don't think the world needs people like me.

Instead of dismissing that thought, I keep it there, in my head, lingering, taunting.

The world doesn't need me.

Dad's calloused hand on my arm startles me awake, and I crank one eye open, just a little, to see him through my blurred vision.

"Son?"

I close my eye again. I can't hold it back today; I can't hide it from Dad any more. It's too much effort and I'm too tired.

Next thing I know I'm being scooped into Dad's arms and he holds me close, so close to his chest, and he rocks me back and forth like I'm a baby, like Mum rocked Cliff last night in her arms while I ate. I think Dad's sitting on the floor, but I can't tell. My head's spinning and stomach churning and I'm lost in my brain, just the faint sounds of a whimpering dog creeping in to accompany the whimpering in my head.

I wake up again, immediately aware that my arm is wrapped around something soft and furry – and bony. I know it's Cliff right away.

I try to open my eyes, but it hurts way too much, so I focus on the warm body of Cliff beside me. His chest rising and falling, his warm breath on my cheek.

I smile, probably only on the inside; I can't really feel my face. But I acknowledge the fact Cliff is here and giving me a feeling that's pretty nice. I even out my own breathing. My stomach still feels weird, but I don't think I've got any more crying in me – at the moment at least. But one thing I definitely do need is a drink. My throat burns.

I inhale deeply and move my arm. It aches, but I bend it and rub at my eyes, removing the sleep and scrubbing away the heaviness. Slowly and gradually, I prise open my eyes, letting the dim light in bit by bit. Though it stings and I can't open them fully, I look around. It's just me and Cliff, the rest of the room empty and quiet, the TV off, blinds drawn. I refocus on Cliff and see his eyes open, looking right at me, his nose pressed up against my cheek. I can even see my reflection in his eyes he's so close. I chuckle, the sound scratchy and faint, as if it's coming from outside.

Cliff moves his head and licks me and I laugh again.

"Hey, Matty."

I look sideways and see Dad, squatting down in front of me, his eyes bloodshot and dark hair sticking up on his head. He doesn't say anything else, just stares at me for a second and then leans forward and plants a kiss on my forehead.

"Water?" he asks as he leans back.

I blink and move my head as much as I can without disturbing Cliff. "Yeah," I croak.

"On it. Try to sit up, yeah?"

I watch him go, orange high-vis, khaki shorts, and bare feet disappearing through the archway and into the kitchen at the back of the house. I hear the water pouring from the tap, and I inhale deeply and push myself up onto my elbow. Cliff joins me, lifting his head and shifting as if he's making room for me to move.

My head's woozy so I pause, pressing it back against the soft sofa, and wait for it to subside. I stare at Cliff, who waits too, looking back at me. His eye looks clean and the sores around his neck and on his body look clean too.

Dad comes back in the room and perches on the floor beside the sofa. He helps me sit up a little more, and I take the glass from his hand and sip, the cold water like new life flowing into my body and soothing my horrible burning throat. After a few minutes, I sigh and hand the glass back to him, and then sink into the cushions. I lift my heavy legs and drag them off the chair, putting my feet on the floor. Cliff stands, waddles forward, and curls up on my lap.

My eyes fill with tears but they're not sad ones.

"Check him out," Dad says, stroking Cliff on the head and smiling at him. "He is one astute animal."

I nod, agreeing. It's like he knows I need him right now.

We sit in silence, both me and Dad looking at and stroking Cliff, sharing the occasional smile. I swallow. "Did you clean his wounds and his eye?" I ask, my voice super croaky still.

"Yes," Dad replies, scratching his beard. "He was pretty hungry, so I fed him and cleaned him up while you slept. Don't worry, I'll show you how to do it all later, when you're ready."

A tear trickles from my eye and I don't even try to stop it.

"Hey, what's up?" Dad asks.

"That's supposed to be my job. I ... I let him down." The water in my tummy curdles.

"Are you kidding?" Dad says. "It's all of our job. We're a family. We're here to help each other." He strokes Cliff's sticky-up ear with his fingertip. "See, even Cliff knows that and he's only been with us a day. You cared for him and now he's caring for you."

Dad's voice is calm and deep and gentle and I nod. He's right. His words are right.

We're here to help each other.

I think back to the comments on Cliff's PicRoll posts, and what Jane told me about being there for her brother, and about the leaflets from the vet about anxiety and depression in dogs.

I fiddle with the friendship band around my wrist, the friendship band Ted gave me, and I think about Ted and how he's always checked in on me, even lately when I've been such a bad mate. I think about Kai and how he forgave me straightaway for totally messing up his birthday.

We're here to help each other.

Good days and bad days.

"Dad," I say, eyes fixed on Cliff's little head, his bald patches and his glittery colourful fur.

"Matt."

"I … I think…"

I don't know how to say it. Because once it's left my mouth it means it's true; it means I've admitted my weakness, how pathetic I truly am. Released all my horrible thoughts into the world, thoughts that will let down Dad and Mum and all my friends, and Cliff.

"Son, you can tell me. Anything. I will always love you." Dad puts a hand on top of mine briefly and then returns it to Cliff's back.

I exhale and say it quickly before I change my mind. "I think I might be depressed."

There. I said it.

The truth is out.

19

Dad doesn't say anything, just leans over Cliff, plunging him into shadow, and places his hand across the back of my neck. He presses his forehead to mine and I hear a small whimper escape his lips.

But it doesn't sound sad. In fact, it sounds like a sigh of relief.

We stay like that for a minute, maybe longer, Cliff still as a statue, curled up on my lap, and I let all the emotion swirl right out of my belly and into the room, not caring that even more tears are falling. I never thought a human, particularly a boy, could produce so much water from their eyes.

Dad eventually leans back, but keeps his hand on my neck. "Never in my life have I been prouder of you than right now."

I frown and look him in the eye.

"What?"

Dad sits back on the floor, wipes his own eyes and drapes his hands over his bent knees. I hadn't realized he'd been crying, and the fact he has makes me feel a little better, a little less pathetic.

"You have no idea how brave you're being by telling me that."

I continue frowning. Brave? Is he for real?

Dad laughs, deep and throaty. "Your expression is a picture right now."

I can't help but laugh, even though the frown stays. "What's brave about me telling you that?"

"Because by telling me that, you're asking for help. And that's a terrifying thing to do sometimes."

I scrunch my hand gently in Cliff's fur. "You think that's true?"

Dad nods. "Yeah, I reckon so." He sighs and sits cross-legged. "We all think we're supposed to just cope with everything thrown at us; life is tough, get over it." He shakes his head. "We all think if we admit we aren't handling things as well as we'd like, as well as we think we should be, that it makes us weak."

I swallow.

"We think it makes us look stronger if we carry on, quietly, like everyone else." Dad shakes his head again, running a hand over his hair. "But it's not true. Not true at all. When you ask for help, you attack one of the darkest, most powerful and evil worries you could ever have: the fear of failure. You look it dead in the eye and you say" – Dad raises a finger and waggles it in the air – "shove off. I need help and I'm not afraid to ask for it."

Cliff lifts his head, face cocked to the side as if he's listening to Dad too. I place my palm on his cheek and rub my thumb up and down his snout.

"That takes more bravery than anything else – admitting that. And that's because we're going face-to-face with ourselves, not another person. Ourselves. Our toughest opponent."

"But I feel so silly because I don't really know what's wrong with me," I say quietly, ashamed. "I … I don't have anything to be, you know, depressed about. I wasn't like this last year, so why now?"

Dad stands, slowly, and sits on the sofa beside me. He exhales, one long breath, and links his hands over his belly. "When Grandad died, I felt like someone had torn out all my insides. Literally. I didn't know how to carry on breathing. He was my best mate."

I keep staring at Cliff the dog and thinking about Grandad Cliff, afraid to look at Dad's sadness.

"I don't know if you remember," he continues, "me not handling it all very well."

I nod. I do remember.

"Well, some days I still don't handle it, to be honest…"

Good days and bad days.

"…but the best thing I ever did was admit that to myself and your mum. Admit that I didn't know how to carry on living without my dad around. Everyone else I knew who'd lost a parent or a family member or friend seemed to be coping, so admitting I wasn't was like admitting I was a failure at life."

"But, Dad, you had a reason to be depressed. Your dad had died." I hate saying the words out loud but at the same time it's how I feel. "I don't have any reason to feel the way I do."

"Son, depression doesn't work like that." Dad pauses, thinking, staring at his crossed feet. "Look, I'm no expert, but I know depression doesn't really care about who it affects. It's pretty ruthless when it comes to choosing who to take down next."

I sigh-laugh, Cliff startling in my lap. "Sorry," I say straightaway, to Dad and Cliff. "I didn't mean to laugh. It's just you make depression out to be a wrestler or something."

Now Dad laughs, placing his hand on Cliff's tummy as he does so. "In a way, I think that's exactly what it is. A wrestler wanting to clothes-line anyone who dares feel deeply enough. I like that." He grins at me.

We sit in silence for a little longer in the soft light of the room, me sipping at my water, Dad tapping his toes together, both of us watching Cliff, even though he's gone back to sleep. I like the fact it's quiet all around me because it's helping the inside of me quieten down too. And I like sitting here, just me and Dad, all the words I've spoken aloud resting between us and no longer inside me.

And then I remember Mum and Dad's conversation, the one I overheard part of from my bedroom.

"Dad?"

"Yes," he replies.

"Did you know? I mean, like, how long did you know I was feeling, you know, like this?" I swivel my purple band round and round my wrist.

"I had my suspicions a while ago. I recognized certain things in your behaviour. The tiredness, all the sleeping. You're such a calm kid but you started to become really irritable. And then there were all the excuses about not playing football."

I gulp.

Football.

He side-eyes me. "But I knew things were getting bad on Saturday when you had your panic attack on the pitch."

I shake my head. "I didn't have a panic attack." He's wrong.

But then I pause, thinking about it, remembering

179

back to Saturday morning, which feels like so long ago. I recall my racing heartbeat, my brain trying to come up with an excuse. I *was* panicking. Now it all makes sense.

"I…" I don't know what to say. I let my head drop into my hand.

Dad's hand touches my knee.

But then I'm hit with a bigger thought. A scarier thought. One that crashes through my brain and spreads fast and heavy to every part of my body.

Mum.

I have to tell all this to Mum.

I tense, my back stiffening.

"What's up?" Dad asks.

"Mum," I whisper through my hand.

"Mum?"

"And football. I'm supposed to go back next week and I have parent consultations coming up and they're going to be terrible. I … I haven't been doing my homework and we've had tests and, and Mum's going to make me get rid of Cliff…"

"Hey, hey, hey," Dad says, placing an arm around my shoulder and pulling me into him. I breathe in his deodorant mixed with the freshly washed smell of his T-shirt. "That won't happen. We love you and we're here to help you."

"But Mum … she doesn't believe kids can get depression. I heard her say it."

Dad lets out another long breath and kisses the top of my head again. He pulls me in even tighter. "Mum … Mum takes a while to get it sometimes. It takes her longer to understand other people's emotions and put herself in other people's shoes. It's not that she doesn't care, because she does. She just says what's in her brain and her heart without thinking it through – probably more than is healthy – but she cares. And you…" He rests his head against the top of mine. "You she loves more than life itself. She'll definitely understand, OK? And I'll be here with you."

I nod into his side, but I'm not sure if it's going to be that simple. I heard what she said. I know how she feels. I don't have *real* problems, regardless of what Dad says about depression not caring for things like that. Dad might think Mum will understand, eventually, but I can't agree.

I press my hand into Cliff's fur and sigh.

20

I sit on the edge of the deck, soles of my feet pressed into the warm grass. The day's overcast; white and grey clouds have bunched up making one giant cloud. I appreciate it though. When Dad made me lunch and forced me to get some fresh air, I didn't feel like dealing with an oppressively happy sun and hot air, but now I'm out here I feel better.

Cliff sits in front of me, staring at my half-eaten cheese sandwich on the small blue plate on my lap. I pat his head between his flat ear and sticky-up one.

"You've had your food," I tell him. His huge eyes, all sparkly and glistening, travel up to meet mine before dropping to the sandwich again. I smile and break off a piece of bread. "OK, just a little bit then. You do need to get stronger." He opens his mouth and I place the piece on the left side, where his remaining teeth are, and he chews once before gulping it down. "Wow. Fast work."

I twirl my phone around in my other hand,

wondering about sending Ted a message. I've been so desperate to tell him about Cliff but the time has never felt right. But then I hear a door squeak open followed by Fifi's yapping as she races down her yard. Cliff stands, his tiny rat-tail curved between his legs, and trots to my left leg. I place my phone on the deck beside my plate and put my hand on his head. Fifi's nose pokes through the fence, and I watch it sniff the air, obviously catching Cliff's scent.

I look down at my dog. "That's the friend I was telling you about. That's Fifi. She's a good girl and I think you'll like her."

Jane appears, peering round the side of her woven patio screen. "Matty!" she says, a big grin lighting her face. "Still not well, my boy?" she enquires, bending down to pick up Fifi, who squirms in her arms.

I shake my head and look down at Cliff. Thank goodness he's here. "I got my dog," I say.

"Oh! Let me see him!" Jane wanders a few steps along the fence-line in her yard, a breeze billowing through her bright pink blouse, which flutters around her. She stops when she can see Cliff cowering by my leg, and her face melts into this weird assortment of expressions. Like happy and sad and "Oh he's so cute" and excited all at once.

"Oh, Matty! Look, Fifi, look." Fifi's tail wags and

she pants, letting out a little bark with her eyes fixed on Cliff.

I carefully scoop up Cliff and hug him close to my chest. He shakes and I hold him tighter. "He's a bit scared at the moment," I say, standing and taking a couple of steps closer to my neighbours.

"I'm sure he is. Bless him. He's been through the mill."

I'm not completely sure what that means but I agree. "But maybe he'll get used to Fifi one day and they'll play." I lift Cliff higher and press his head into my neck and under my chin, lapping up his warmth and softness.

"Oh yes. Maybe I'll come over on my own to get him used to my scent first." Jane presses her nose to Fifi's. She then looks at me, this strange smile on her face, which thins her lips and her eyes. "We have a little present inside for him, a couple of tennis balls and some chicken treats."

"Thank you," I say, my voice quiet as a wave of emotion washes over me.

"You know, I think you will make a big difference to Cliff's life, Matty," Jane says. "Dogs need others to help them mend, exactly like humans, and I think Cliff has found the person to nurse him through this next part of his life."

I nod and smile.

"He will probably always have a few problems, but he has you to show him that it's OK, that he's safe now. And he has me and Fifi to help when he's ready."

Breathing in Cliff's dog smell, I nod again, knowing that's exactly what I will do: make sure Cliff knows he is always safe with me, bad day or good day. I feel a few tears well behind my closed eyes but I'm saved by Dad stepping onto the deck, his footsteps thudding along the wood. It's like he's making a loud arrival on purpose.

"Afternoon, Jane," he says, coming to stand beside me. He puts a hand on my shoulder and squeezes reassuringly.

I'm here for Cliff – and Dad's here for me.

"Brian, I was just saying how lucky Cliff is to have Matty taking care of him now," Jane says, running a hand through Fifi's white fluff from the top of her head along to her back.

"I dunno, Jane," Dad replies. "I'd say we're the lucky ones to have Cliff." Our eyes meet and he winks.

"Well, that too!" Jane laughs.

"Maybe take him inside now," Dad says, giving me the break I need to escape.

"It's been lovely to meet you, Cliff, and lovely to see you, Matt." Jane waves goodbye to us with Fifi's paw, and I do as Dad says and head inside. "And remember, I can come over and look after him any time you need me, just like I used to come over and look after you, Matty, until you got so grown up."

"Thanks," I reply, stepping into the coolness of the kitchen, just catching Jane asking Dad something about cutting back trees.

I sigh and head into the lounge, easing into the leather sofa. With a belly that's filled partly with sandwich and the remainder with nerves, I lie down on my side, tired again. I rest my head on my Wolves cushion, nestling Cliff in the crook of my arm, and close my eyes. His soft fur feels like velvet on my cheek and calms my breathing.

Not long until Mum comes home. Not long until I have to tell her all the things I've told Dad. I have Dad's understanding, I know that, but I want my mum too. I want her to understand like Dad does, to not tell me I'm silly or to cheer up. I realize now that if it were that easy, if she was right and mind over matter really was the answer, I'd have done it by now and wouldn't have spent the last few months feeling like I have.

And I need to tell her that I'm not ready to return to football. Not next week, not next month. Maybe not for the rest of the year.

I can't do this.

I hear the back door slide closed and Dad pad into the lounge, the smell of coffee accompanying him. I open one eye and peer at him, and he smiles back.

"You good?" he asks, sitting back on the lounger opposite with a black mug in his hand.

I exhale through my nose, wondering whether to tell him.

"Worried about talking to Mum still?"

I glance at him. "Yeah, a bit."

"I know. She seems tough on the outside, but she's soft really. Softer than me probably, and that's why she hides it. So she doesn't get hurt. Want me to talk to her first?" he asks, sipping his coffee.

Do I? I heard how their last conversation went, when Dad tried to talk to Mum about his concerns for me. And it wasn't good. But really, will the words coming from *me* this time make her listen? I chew the inside of my mouth, dread eating up every one of my brain cells.

"Or we do it together?"

All those people who responded to Cliff, telling him, and me, that with a little help we can do it, we can overcome the bad stuff and start to heal. It's help I'm giving Cliff to heal and it's help Dad's offering me.

I'll take it.

"OK, yeah, together," I reply.

"Together."

21

Mum and Dad potter about the kitchen, Mum making herself a cup of chai tea like she always does when she gets in from work and Dad preparing dinner like he always does on his nights to cook.

Mum waltzed through the door at 4.30 p.m., left her red bag on the stairs and kicked off her flip-flops at the door – exactly like she always does. She said hello to me, kissed me on the head – as well as giving Cliff a kiss – and asked me a few questions about school. Dad interrupted, wanting her to check to see if the chicken thighs in the fridge were still OK to cook.

Dad to the rescue – again.

Everything about my house, about right now, looks and sounds exactly like it normally does at this time of day; even Cliff being here is the most normal thing ever. The carpet underneath my legs and bum where I sit trying to get Cliff to play with his Winnie the Pooh toy. The wall-hung TV, the sports channel, the green of the football pitch and the enthusiastic chatter of the commentators. The afternoon sun breaking through the sea of clouds, lighting up the green of our front yard and exposing the fingerprints on our glass doors.

But it doesn't feel it. Not inside my head and my heart and my belly.

Because nothing is normal.

And nothing will ever be normal again.

It's like I'm numb, everything underneath my skin frozen solid with fear and panic.

Dad showed me how to breathe if I felt my chest tightening: deep breaths in through my nose and out through my mouth, filling up my chest and stomach as much as possible. I've been doing that, and it does help, but I'm still not sure I can do this.

I can't do this.

I can't do this.

But I have to.

Cliff lifts a paw as I swipe Winnie past him, like he's reaching out to stop it. He misses, too late, but still looks so cute and I'm so proud of him for trying. It feels like a breakthrough. We slept a few hours after lunch, and this is the first time I've been able to play with him. He didn't much like the squeaky hotdog toy or fake, soft tennis ball, but the minute I grabbed Winnie out of his bed I swear his tail did that small wag thing. So, since then, I've sat on the floor, alternating between watching Cliff and the TV, listening for Mum's car to pull up and wondering why this is happening to me.

Mum comes into the lounge, Dad right behind her. I glance to him and he gives me a long, reassuring look.

This is it. It's time.

They both sit on the two-seater, Mum doing her usual grunt noise to announce how happy she is to take the weight off her feet finally. Mum *does* work hard and *is* on her feet all day. I should probably not be so annoyed with her when she makes that sound.

"So, do I get to book parent consultations yet? Next week, aren't they?"

That's a lot of questions all at once and my brain isn't sending any clear messages to my mouth. I stay mute, continuing to drag the bear back and forth in front of Cliff. He tracks its movements with his eyes, occasionally lifting his paw again. I don't think he's ever had someone to play with him before. But now he does and he's learning what to do.

"Matthew?" Mum says in a sing-song voice, and I look up at her. "School? Consultations?" Then she frowns, eyes drifting all over my face.

"Nat, not now. Maybe later, yeah?"

She frowns again, looks from Dad to me. "What's going on?" she asks, leaning back into the creaking chair. "You're frightening me."

190

I soak up Dad's calmness, his gentle expression, his kind eyes. I study Cliff, watch how he's learning how to live again, but live properly this time.

I suck in my breath.

"Mum." In through my nose, out through my mouth.

She doesn't reply, just stares at me, mouth agape.

"Mum, I... I didn't go to school today because I don't think I'm very well," I start.

"O–K..." she answers, the frown coming back to crinkle her forehead, the circles under her eyes suddenly looking darker than ever. Her eyes are still flitting between me and Dad, expectant.

I scrunch Winnie in my fist, my eyes starting to burn. "And I've... I think that..."

I stop and breathe again.

I can't do this.

But I'm braver than I believe.

Cliff couldn't ask for help, but I can. And I have to. I need *both* my parents.

"Mum, my brain isn't very well. I think I might be depressed."

And it's done.

The world falls silent. Mum doesn't move, just stares at me, eyes narrowed. Dad stares at Mum, his eyes wide.

Cliff climbs onto my legs, circles a couple of times,

his paw pads cool on my hot skin, and plonks down. His head rests against my belly, his back paws touching his front paws where they're bent up.

I place my hand on him, chewing the inside of my cheek until I taste blood.

"Right." Mum finally speaks, her rigid body relaxing. "Right," she says again, nodding at me, a strange sad smile on her lips.

I catch Dad's eye and he nods at me.

"So…" Mum takes a sip of tea and crosses her legs, and I can see her mind working overtime. "What makes you say that?"

I glance at her, her eyes fixed on Cliff in my lap. I stroke Cliff, composing myself. And I start. I mention not doing my homework, about forgetting things and not wanting to go out with my friends. I talk about football and not enjoying it any more, and how I feel like I'm letting everyone down all the time, of what a useless friend and son I am and what a waste of space I am.

"Oh, Matty, don't say silly things—"

"No, Nat." Dad places a hand on Mum's arm. "Please don't tell Matthew he's being silly. Please don't do that. He's opening up to you right now." Dad's voice is quiet but firm, and for once Mum doesn't cut him off or talk over him.

I think I've knocked the wind out of her.

She nods, smiles a small smile, and I inhale again.

In through the nose.

"I'm no use to anyone."

I close my eyes, letting my head flop forward. Tiredness and exhaustion swoop down on me like a peregrine falcon and all I want to do is sleep. I feel arms envelop me, Dad's arms, and I hear Mum sniffling and taking deep breaths over and over, still in her chair. I didn't mean to make her feel sad, to make her cry. "Oh, Matthew. I… I…"

"Sorry," I whisper, squeezing my eyes tightly closed. "I'm so sorry."

"Matty … no …" But all I hear then is her sniff and cry and breathe heavily again.

"No, mate, you have nothing to be sorry for." Dad's voice is nasal, like he has a cold. "We love you so much, buddy." He holds me tighter and I let my arms droop to my sides, every ounce of energy zapped and spent.

"I'm tired," I whisper.

"Come on then, let's get you up to bed."

Dad gathers Cliff into one arm and helps me stand with the other. I sway, my balance off, and open my eyes.

"Matty, I love you. Please know that I love you," Mum says, her voice muffled. From the corner of my eye I see her face buried in her hands, her body all curled up on the chair. She suddenly looks so small, as if I've broken the strong walls that keep her standing. But Dad leads me away, towards the stairs, and we climb slowly. He tucks me into bed with Cliff beside me and pulls down my blind. With a kiss on my forehead, he whispers into my temple, then turns, leaves and shuts the door.

I didn't react but I heard what he said.

"I'm so proud of you, son."

22

Twenty-four hours I've been in my bed, apart from peeing and drinking and nibbling at the food my parents have brought me. Cliff's sleeping in his bed now on my bedroom floor, all snuggled in his bone blanket. Dad must have brought that up while I slept too. I think my dog's as tired as me! Maybe we could win some kind of sleeping award. I wonder if that's even a thing.

I peel the covers off me and sit up slowly, my body sore. Sleeping all night and day is more tiring than playing a game of football. I chuckle, because that makes zero sense.

I drag a hand down my face and then stretch. My muscles pull and strain but I think I'm all slept out. Cliff continues to sleep, his tiny little chest and belly moving in a steady and relaxed rhythm. He's so cute and fragile and, though I've only known him less than a week, I absolutely love him.

After a few minutes of staring at Cliff, I reach over

and grab my phone off my bedside table, switch it on and type in the pass code. As expected there are loads of unread messages and my stomach turns over with guilt. I should let my friends know I'm OK, that I'm alive and well – which I guess is a lie now that I think about it. I wonder if they'll understand. But I know straightaway they will. I would if it was one of them. I know I would.

Ted: Mate?

Ted: Hope you're not feeling too bad.

Ted: Matt?

Kai: Seriously dude get in touch.

I smile to myself, feeling pretty lucky to have such good mates. I'll reply soon, when my head's not so sleepy. I swipe to PicRoll, opening Cliff's second to last post.

I sit forward.

What the what?

11,523 likes and 2,369 comments.

That can't be right.

But it is. It's definitely right, and I watch as the numbers continue to increase. There's no way I can read through all these comments. If only Cliff could read, he'd be able to help me respond to everyone.

Help. There's that word again.

Maybe I could ask my friends to help. Ask Ted and Kai if they'll read and respond to the comments.

Maybe. They don't know about Cliff. Maybe the reason I haven't told them yet is also part of my … depression. I swallow down the word.

I scroll through a couple of the top comments, my heart squidging up then growing with each kind word.

You're my hero!

Literally THE cutest darn dog in the universe.

Great that you found someone who loves you.

People are sharing photos of their own rescue dogs, telling me – telling Cliff – about how much they love them. Some comments are even from other accounts owned by the dog itself. It's … it's brilliant! The love pouring out of people for Cliff is incredible and makes my heart melt. I glance down at him and grin at how oblivious he is that all this love is for him. I mean, I'm taking some of it too but he's the real reason.

I close the post and open the next one, the one where Cliff says he wants to help me.

There are even more likes and comments on this

one, but this time they're mainly for me or both me and Cliff. *Me.* I shake my head and start reading.

Sending all my love to you, Cliff, and your boy too.

Your boy is a fighter, just like you!

So sad to hear you think he's suffering. Make sure he reaches out and asks for help.

There are so many posts similar to these, and others just with one or lots of hearts and hug emojis. And then I read another.

Whatever it is, I think your boy has the biggest heart, and people with big hearts tend to find life the toughest. He'll get through it, especially with you by his side.

I close down my phone and shift to sit sideways, facing Cliff. He's awake, big goofy eyes staring up at me from his comfy nest.

"People think we're going to be fine," I say to him. "I hope they're right."

Cliff lifts his head and tilts it to the side, and then he sneezes. I snort-laugh and put my fingertips to my lips quickly, nervous that I might have scared him. But he doesn't startle. Instead, his tail wags, not once but a few times.

I climb out of bed and gently scoop him into my arms, kissing him over and over on his head.

And then I hear three knocks at the front door and my stomach swirls.

Ted's here.

What's Ted doing here? My clock tells me it's 5.15 p.m. and aromas of whatever Mum's cooking float in under my door. I strain to hear the voices murmuring downstairs and then wait, unsure what to do.

Two light taps on my door and Dad pokes his head through.

"Ah, good, you're awake. Ted's here." Dad opens the door wider and steps in.

I look down at myself, at the same now-crumpled shorts and shirt I had on when we went to pick Cliff up from the vet. Wow, I must stink. I can't believe I've been in the same clothes since Wednesday.

"You look fine, mate," Dad says, crouching beside me and stroking Cliff.

"Thanks for taking care of Cliff the last couple of days."

"I told you, he's family now."

"How's Mum?"

Dad pauses, then says, "She's fine. Lots of emotions coming out. But don't worry about Mum at the moment. She'll talk to you properly soon. Come down and see your friends."

"Friends? Who else is here?"

"There's Kai and Joseph."

I screw up my face. *Joseph?* "As in football Joseph?"

"The very same."

What's he doing here?

"Come on."

I sigh and stand, holding Cliff just a little tighter, hoping he'll protect me – and cover up my stinky creased clothes. At least if my friends do say I smell I can blame it on Cliff.

Dad and I head down the stairs, and at the bottom I see my two friends and, yeah, definitely Joseph sitting in the lounge, shoes off, and each of them perched on the edge of the chairs.

"I'll leave you to it," Dad says, and he strides off to join Mum in the kitchen.

Joseph stands as I walk into the lounge, taking off his cap and holding it to his chest the same way I'm holding Cliff.

"OMG is that a dog?" Kai comes straight over, his red cap pulled low over his face the way he usually wears it.

"Yeah, this is Cliff, but you have to be quiet and slow because he's a bit scared of everything."

Kai immediately tiptoes the final few steps, and I notice Ted following him. They both peer at Cliff, their faces scrunched with concern as their eyes travel all over Cliff's body.

"What happened to him?" Ted says, his voice low.

"We're not sure but we found him tied up in the park on Sunday with this note saying he was ugly and sad."

"No way!" Kai says, his eyebrows rising.

"He looks much better than he did." I smile, kissing Cliff on the head.

My friends are silent for a minute, clearly taking it all in.

"Can I pat him?" Ted asks, moving his hand forward a little. I nod and Ted carefully touches Cliff's head with his fingertips. "He's so cute." Ted smiles.

"Hello, little one," Kai says. "I'm sorry you were abandoned."

"Wait a second…" We all turn as Joseph speaks. He puts his cap back on his head and pulls his mobile from his pocket, tapping on his screen. He finds whatever he's looking for, and then, holding it out, he comes over. "Is this him?"

I look past Ted and Kai and see Cliff on Joseph's screen – the photos I added on PicRoll. I swallow, realizing what this means: they're going to see the last post; they're going to know who the boy with problems is.

I freeze, eyes bouncing from Ted to Kai and then to Joseph.

What is he doing here anyway? He never comes to my house.

Joseph puts his phone back in his pocket and takes off his cap again, his hair not looking quite so perfect right now.

"It's OK," he says with a small grin. "I can't believe it's the same dog, your dog. But it all makes sense. I was right."

I stare hard at Joseph, trying to work out what he means, what's going on in his head.

Joseph turns and goes back to the sofa, plopping down heavily. Ted and Kai follow, glancing at me with frowns on their faces. I follow too, but slower, my footsteps nervous and my heart beating fast.

In through my nose. Out through my mouth.

"Like, don't tell anyone or anything, OK, like totally promise you won't spill." Joseph looks to each of us, eyes wide and pleading. I see something familiar in his expression now.

"Yeah, totally," Kai says.

"Same," Ted agrees.

"Promise," I add. "What is it?"

Joseph sighs and leans back, twisting his cap in his hands. "I'd never tell my other mates. Man, they'd eat me alive. I wanted to talk to you at football when you … you know, and at school the other day. Actually for a while, but…" He shrugs. "You know how it is."

I don't. Though my fast-beating heart suggests maybe I do.

Joseph runs a hand through his hair. "But … well … since I lost my dad I've had to see someone about my anxiety."

I lower my knees onto the soft carpet, holding Cliff nice and close. I did not expect that.

"And when I saw you the other day, at football, I kind of knew something was wrong. You know, something like what happens to me." He looks at me, eyes holding my gaze. "I have anxiety attacks quite a lot. Talking definitely helps, but, like, it can be pretty bad some days."

I don't nod or speak, just stare back, a flood of thoughts and emotions all battling for control of my brain. But one comes through loud and clear.

Good days and bad days.

"You don't have to say anything. I follow a lot of posts on PicRoll about anxiety and stuff – it helps me feel less alone and weird – and that's why I know about Cliff the Abandoned Dog. I can't believe he's yours, but it all adds up now. I get the feeling you might suffer like me, or maybe a bit different but also the same."

He shrugs again. I can see his discomfort and this is not the same Joseph I've always known. I'm starting to realize how many people there are who hide their emotions and true selves so they can appear tough. Mum included.

No words. Still no words. Not from me or Ted.

But Kai speaks. "Man, seriously?"

Joseph nods.

"And that's why you wanted to come over to see Matt? That's why you suggested it?" Ted says, scratching his forehead, his black friendship band sliding up and down his arm.

"Yeah, I don't know if I'm … erm … welcome, and like maybe you don't want to talk about it or anything, and I totally get that, but I wanted you to know that I can help, and stuff. If you need it. I wish I had friends who understood…" Joseph trails off.

I've read about characters' jaws dropping but have never really known what that means – until now. Now I get it. Because my jaw has properly dropped.

I realize I'm staring at him, Ted and Kai too, and I cough to clear my throat, blinking a few times. All these years I've known Joseph and always saw him as tough and cool, but it seems he's an expert at hiding. "I appreciate it, thanks," I say. "And same. You can always talk to me. Us. We won't tell anyone."

Joseph nods and puts his cap back on his head.

"And, well, thanks for being so honest and telling us all that stuff," I add, thinking about Dad being proud of me for sharing.

He nods again.

"So, is it true?" Ted asks me. "Is Joseph right?"

"About what?" I ask.

"You know, about the anxiety." He clasps his hands in his lap, peering at me with sad eyes.

Well, if Joseph can be honest and has had the heart to come round here to see me, I guess I can do it too.

"Er, kind of. But, not anxiety, I don't think anyway. I … I might be depressed."

The word still feels alien on my tongue, something I don't deserve to use, but I need to get used to hearing it said about me. I hug Cliff, focusing on his fur, waiting for them to laugh at me or whatever – I already know they won't.

"Man, I'm sorry," Kai says, breaking the silence.

I look up at him and smile. "It's me that needs to say that," I reply. "I let you guys down big time – you know, the whole birthday party thing" – I look at Joseph and Ted – "and all the dropping out of the football matches. I'm so embarrassed thinking about it." I shake my head, my cheeks hot. Forcing those memories out will make me cry but I am *not* going to cry now.

"Nah, nothing to be embarrassed about," Ted says. "And nothing to be sorry about. I mean, I'm sorry I didn't notice. I feel bad about it."

"Same," Kai adds.

"No one needs to feel sorry," Joseph says. "Depression is the worst – my mum has it. Some days she's the best person in the world, happy and fun, just like she used to be before we lost Dad." He twists his cap some more, head down, watching it. "And then on others, it's like this big black cloud hangs over her head and pours so much rain on her that she can't see anything but rain." He glances up. "That's how she describes it, anyway. It was a way to make me and my sister understand."

I cannot get over how much Joseph is telling us. His anxiety, his mum's depression. And I do feel proud of him.

"Is that how it is for you, the rain-cloud thing?" Ted asks, glancing at me.

I nod. "Yeah, I think it's the perfect way to describe it." I roll onto my backside, putting Cliff down on the floor between my legs. "Some moments I feel fine, and I wonder why I've been acting so miserable and weird on the other days, but then it's like nothing's right and I don't want to do anything or talk to anyone and I just want to sleep."

Joseph nods, and Ted and Kai glance at each other and then at me.

"I never used to be like this so I guess I've tried to carry on, you know, pretending I'm OK, hoping it will go away."

"That's heavy," Kai says. "But can you ... will you get some help now?"

I shrug, not really sure what happens next. I need to talk to Mum.

Dad appears at the archway, drying his hands with a dishcloth. "You fellas want a drink or snack?"

Joseph stands, wedging his cap on his head. "No thanks, Mr Brown," he says, more polite than I have ever heard him speak before. "My mum's cooking and I should get going."

Kai and Ted both stand too. "No thanks," they say at the same time, and the three of them edge towards the front door.

"OK, well, thanks for coming over," Dad says, and turns, bouncing his eyebrows up and down at me just once.

I stand, leaving Cliff lying on the floor, and go with my friends to the hallway.

"Bye, Cliff," Kai says, waving to him.

"Look after my best mate, yeah?" Ted says to Cliff, and Cliff cocks his head to the side, as if he's really listening. "Awww," Ted says. "He's so cute."

"Brilliant dog, by the way," Joseph says. "And don't worry, I won't tell anyone that he's PicRoll Cliff."

I nod. "Thanks, Joseph. And, you know, thanks for telling me about you and your mum, and for coming over like you have. I think you're really brave."

Joseph pats me on the shoulder, grinning. "Any time, mate."

Ted and Kai pat me too, and I say goodbye to them, closing the door as they head off down the path and disappear into the early evening darkness.

I turn and lean back against the door, my head stuffed full and churning with new knowledge and thoughts, but my heart feeling stronger than it has in days.

23

The door swings open and Mum and Dad step out of the therapist's room, followed by Dr Helen Bowers in her brown trouser suit and black heels. I bolt to my feet, my heart like a drill in my chest, and Helen gives me a thumbs-up. "Nice to meet you, Matthew. Until next week, and you all have my number in the meantime."

"You too," I reply, my cheeks burning. I have to come back and talk to her about me and all my feelings and stuff, and right now I am not looking forward to that. Yeah, Helen's nice, and smart, and she didn't press me for that much information, but the fact I have to talk to a psychologist every week for a while makes me feel super weird.

But then everything is weird right now, especially now I know about Joseph and his mum, and about all the other people who've been reaching out and telling me and Cliff about their problems on PicRoll and how they wouldn't be here if it wasn't for their psychologists.

Depression and anxiety are way more common than I realized, and not just in adults, but in kids and animals too. I think me speaking to a psychologist is going to take some getting used to.

Helen shakes Mum's and Dad's hands and then waves at the three of us, before disappearing back into her room, closing the door quietly behind her.

And here we are. Me and Mum and Dad.

It's been over two weeks since I told Mum about everything and, though she hasn't really mentioned the D word, we've hugged and cried and talked heaps. I remember what Dad said about Mum needing time to figure it out for herself and I understand. It's taken me months to realize I have mental health issues. She needs time and help too.

Those words will also take some getting used to.

I look up at my parents. Breathe in through the nose, out through the mouth. I have no idea what they've discussed with Helen, though it was obviously about me. I realize my parents are affected just as much as me by my depression. They said that all the things I told them were the hardest things they've ever heard, and that I should be here and they'll do anything and everything they can to help me believe that. I hope the chat with Helen helped Mum understand a bit more too. She's seemed so fragile and I feel bad. It's me who broke her down, but knowing she's here for me, Dad too, gives me the strength I need.

Mum passes her red bag to Dad, and he takes it, eyes still fixed on me. They both dressed smart for the meeting; Mum more so than Dad. He's in his usual green shorts, but instead of a T-shirt and flip-flops he swapped them for a black collared shirt and his smart black runners. Mum on the other hand looks beautiful, wearing her favourite black-and-white-striped dress that comes down to her ankles and flows out every time she takes a step.

She takes a few of those steps closer to me now, to where I stand in front of the row of cushioned seats in the waiting area. But these are small steps and she's looking down at her hands as they smooth out the creases in her dress.

I peer up at her face, trying to gauge how she's feeling, and I gasp at the tears dripping from her eyes.

"Mum?" I say, closing the gap between us. "What's wrong?"

She lifts her head, black make-up merging with her tears, and gives me a painful smile. She spreads her arms and wraps me up in a hug – the biggest, cuddliest, most loving hug I think my mum has ever given me.

Emotions come thick and fast, battering me. But the main one is relief. I don't cry though. It could be that

I've run out of tears – finally. I squeeze Mum back, my head on her shoulder because I'm not far off her height now. She rests her head on mine.

"You, Matthew Archibald Brown, are the most incredible and bravest kid I have ever known, and I am the proudest mother in the whole universe." She grabs my shoulders and pushes me back, blinking fast as she stares at my face. "Do you hear me? The proudest mother. And also the sorriest. I love you and I am so ashamed of my behaviour." She drags me back into her embrace before I have a chance to speak.

Dad joins us, wrapping one arm around each of us. "Stop being hard on yourself," he starts, but I feel Mum shaking her head where it rests on mine.

"No, not this time. I haven't listened when I should have. I haven't let Matty, or you, feel whatever you want to feel, or let you react the way you want to. I always think I know best about how you should be feeling about things, or that you should just feel the way I do. That's wrong of me, but I am going to do so much better." She sniffs and lets out a small laugh. "I mean it, you two. So much better, I promise. It's OK to stop sometimes and allow ourselves to be sad or tired or confused. I know that now. I've always known it, but I need to learn how to do so – for me and you."

We hug some more, and I believe her. Helen says it won't be easy, and that it could be that I never *don't* have depression – which scares me more than I can put into words. But she says that depression is something that can be controlled as long as I stay honest with myself about how I feel and start to recognize my behaviours when I'm spiralling – her word – into depression.

I admit the whole thing terrifies me, and sometimes I feel OK and am convinced I can't possibly have depression, not truly, but one thing I know is that I don't want to feel the way I have been any more. I don't want my friends or my parents to suffer – and I don't want to suffer.

I'm ready.

Outside in the clinic car park, Dad unlocks Mum's car with a beep and we climb in out of the hot, sunny afternoon air. He starts the engine, and both Mum and Dad peer round their headrests at me as I fasten my seatbelt.

"What?" I ask.

"Nothing," they say at the same time.

"Let's go home and see that beautiful dog of yours, right?" Mum says. "Ted and Kai will be round in about an hour too."

"Definitely." It's Friday, and even though Ted has a football match tomorrow, he's allowed to sleep over tonight, Kai too. I actually can't wait to play some *Jungle Warfare* with them and for them to see Cliff again.

My insides feel warm.

Going home and knowing Cliff is there – under the watchful eye of Jane, of course – and that he might want to play with his Winnie the Pooh toy, sends a shiver of excitement through me. He hasn't barked yet and still isn't quite ready to play with Fifi, but one day at a time.

Mum turns on the radio to Sam Cooke singing "Wonderful World" again, and this time I don't try to block out the lyrics.

"No!" I flop my head back onto my Wolves cushion propped behind me.

"Yes! The reigning champion wins again!" Kai shoves my shoulder and I laugh, falling sideways.

"You have all the luck," I tell him, rolling my eyes.

"Not luck, my friend," Kai says. "Pure skill."

We're camped out in the lounge, *Jungle Warfare* set up on the TV. We've spread the pillows, sleeping bags, blankets and cushions that Mum brought downstairs all over the floor as this is where we're sleeping tonight. Ted's awake, but already cuddled up under the blankets since he has that game tomorrow.

It's about midnight, the house quiet, Mum and Dad in bed. We're keeping our voices down, not just because of the time, but also because of Cliff.

I glance over at him, where he's curled up in his bed, the Winnie the Pooh toy under his chin. His eyes are open, watching us, but he seems calm. I reach over and give him a stroke and a pat and he sighs.

"Aw," Kai says. "I love it when he sighs."

I nod. I do too.

Ted props his head onto one hand. "So, do you think you'll come to watch the game tomorrow?"

It's my turn to sigh. I chew the inside of my cheek and place my controller down beside me. Ted texted about coming along to watch the Whales earlier in the week, but I'm still not sure. "I don't know."

"That's cool," Ted says. "Maybe next time. I know the team would be happy to see you, but when you're ready."

I smile, grateful to have him as a friend. "Yeah, maybe next time."

"Are you feeling, you know, OK?" Kai asks, stretching out his legs.

"You can talk to us if you want to," Ted adds.

"Thanks, that means a lot." And I mean it. "I feel OK, to be honest. Like, I'm pleased I'm not keeping all the feelings inside me as much, but confused. I still don't really understand why I'm like this."

We fall silent for a bit, all of us no doubt wondering the answer to this. Though I'm starting to accept there isn't one, and that's OK too.

I place my hand on Cliff's back, something I've found myself doing a lot when I talk about my depression. "But, I reckon having all you guys, the psychologist, and Dad and Mum, things will be OK. I just need to learn more about it all, keep sharing and asking for help when I need it."

"You can do that with us," Ted says.

"Definitely," Kai says.

"Thanks." I'm seriously lucky to have these two.

Kai slides back and grabs his phone out of his bag. "I forgot to say, I started following Cliff's PicRoll account. I can't believe how popular it is."

"I know, right?" I say, also reaching for my phone on the sofa behind me. "I honestly can't believe so many people are interested in his story. And mine."

"Have you posted anything new?" Ted asks, laying his head back down on a blue pillow.

"No, not this week. I've been..." I shrug, not sure what I've been. All the talks and hugs and tears with Mum and Dad, not to mention heaps more sleep, have left me pretty empty. And I decided to come clean. Told them I'd set up an account just for Cliff. It was weird, but Mum read through the posts and didn't get cross at all, not like I expected. She said she was pleased I'd done it, proud of me in fact – though not so much that I'd lied about my age. She even offered to help reply to comments in the future. I'm so glad I'm not holding in any more secrets, that's for sure.

Ted and Kai don't seem to expect me to finish the sentence anyway, which I appreciate. Sometimes the right words don't come. Sometimes I don't think there are any right words. Silence works just as well.

And then I have an idea. I've taken tons of photos of Cliff these past few days. It's hard not to when he's so cute all the time.

"Want to help me reply to all the comments and maybe write the next Cliff post?"

Ted sits up again and Kai's eyebrows rise.

"Are you serious?" Kai asks.

"Yeah, of course," I say, nodding.

"That would be awesome," Ted says.

"Too right," Kai adds.

I laugh, grateful again, and surprised by their enthusiasm. Cliff lifts his head and looks at me, his big golf-ball eyes shining in the light from the TV. I lean forward and press my nose to his wet one, then kiss him on the head. As I move my face away, he licks my nose and my heart melts. "Thanks, buddy," I whisper.

This is me today. See how good I look, trotting about MY yard.

Look at how my skin and fur and eye have healed up. I'm like a new dog. And I am so happy! But the best thing, the best thing in the whole wide world, is, because of all of your love, his best friends and parents, but mainly because my boy asked for help, he's feeling better about his problems too.

He's ready to take on the world. Well, maybe not the whole world.

But isn't that the coolest thing?

We're both getting better, together, and I never ever want to be anywhere else but by his side.

AUTHOR NOTE

Dear Reader,

Depression is one scary word and an even scarier topic! Just saying the word out loud terrifies even the toughest of people. There's so much I want to include in this author note, but knowing where to start and how to say it is trickier than I expected. I'm no expert, but I'll try my best – no one can ever ask for more than that.

The D word affects many of us across the world, young and old. Yet frustratingly a large amount of people still don't take it seriously enough or believe it's even real. They think it's a type of sadness – which it very much isn't. And many only accept it as suffering in those who've experienced an obvious or dramatic trauma. Of course, depression doesn't work that way. It never has and never will.

When I was diagnosed with depression, initially I was angry. Disappointed in myself that I could be so weak to think and feel the way I was. I'd had a happy and fun life filled with opportunities and love and support. Surely someone as lucky as me had the tools to fight through a silly little phase? All I had to do was read the newspaper or watch the TV to see real suffering – right? That should fix it.

This attitude and approach, which we've all heard or even offered, only leads to more and more unnecessary pressure on a pair of already broken shoulders.

As I healed, or rather continue to heal, I realized that admitting and accepting I was unwell was the real starting point. Asking for help was what ultimately saved me from the darkest of places. But then I began wondering about other people. About how many children there were struggling with self-hate, an unexplainable lack of enthusiasm, and often intrusive thoughts; how many of them were without the words or knowledge to understand how they felt. How many were afraid to talk for fear of ridicule, or that they'd be dismissed and told to cheer up, or who had caring family, friends and teachers who simply didn't have the understanding themselves.

The idea for *The Bravest Word* was born from having two dogs who teach me every day to stop and climb out of my head. It's a raw, truthful story that shows how depression takes hold, how it weaves into everything we do, tricks us, and how, before we know, it can drag us into its all-consuming vacuum. Yet, I want you to know that with the right support and an understanding ear, we can all learn to open up and to listen, to share our true feelings without fear of judgement, and maybe then take steps to recover and live a fulfilling life.

Being afraid is OK. Bravery is acting despite your fear. And asking for help is bravery in its purest, most vulnerable form.

Kate

xx

ACKNOWLEDGEMENTS

I find acknowledgements hard to write because I am beyond lucky to have so many amazing people in my life; so there's a real sharp-edged fear of WHAT IF I FORGET TO THANK SOMEONE? So, I'm going to do my absolute best to remember and thank all the people who read early versions of this book, supported me throughout the process and helped bring this special little story to life. (P.S. If I have forgotten you, I'm sorry and don't hate me.)

First up, I have to thank my beloved and wonderful publisher, Linsay Knight. How blessed I am to have become a part of Team Walker while Linsay was at the helm! Having worked with Linsay over the past couple of years on several projects, her belief in me as a writer (and person) has given me confidence in myself that I lack so very much. All those emails I sent her, all my worries and concerns I unloaded and she absorbed … what a legend. I will miss working with you so much, Linsay! And of course, a big thank you to Clare Hallifax for taking over the controls and believing in me and my work. I'm looking forward to working with you in the future!

Also, a massive thank you to Kristina Schulz, my patient and dedicated editor. This was our first adventure together and what a lucky author I am! I was told Kristina was outstanding and hardworking before we met and this turned out to be incredibly accurate. Smart, sweet, funny, brilliant. Thank you, Kristina. I can't wait to work on the next one with you!

Massive thanks to the other members of Team Walker: the amazing Sarah Davis who brings to life my characters as if she lives inside my brain; Maraya, my publicist, as well as Georgie and Beth. To Steve, Janine, Jarred and the amazing Angela Van Den Belt. You make up the best team an author could ask for.

The biggest of thanks to Frances Taffinder, Jenny Bish and Denise Johnstone-Burt at Walker UK for your passion and belief in this story, and me. You are incredible people! To Rebecca J Hall and Faith Leung for your impressively fancy skills; to Thy Bui for such an extraordinary and stunning UK cover illustration; and to everyone in the PR, Marketing and Sales teams for all the tireless work you do.

A heartfelt thank you to my agent, Chloe Davis, who responds in the most polite and timely manner to, quite frankly, the unhealthy number of emails I send her. What a rock she's become. A true professional. I must also mention the lovely Clare Wallace, who kindly accepted, considered and passed to Chloe my highly unusual query letter for this book. You both welcomed me into the Darley Anderson Children's Agency of which I'm so honoured to be a part.

I have to thank all the early readers who volunteered to wade through this book and provide me with the best feedback – as well as all the gushing and the compliments and the encouragement. Including my writing love Judy Roberts, Dee White, Kate Gordon, Pamela Freeman, Meagan Dallner, Lara Lillibridge, Karen Rosenburg, Emma Norris, JC Davis, Nicole Bezanson and Kimberly Fernando. I often return to your emails, especially on the days when imposter syndrome visits, just to read your words. Your support is ongoing.

A big thank you to my mum, who reads all my work and provides the best proud mummy pats on the back! Fist bumps to my kids and husband who put up with my weirdness and daydreaming, the large number of take-outs we consume when I'm drafting, and for loving me even though I rarely change out of my pyjamas.

Thanks to all the dedicated booksellers, teachers, librarians, parents, guardians, book reviewers and all of you fabulous book-loving peeps for putting this book in the hands of children. Of course big thanks to my readers, and dare I say fans. I can't thank you enough for taking the time to meet Matty and Cliff, diving into their world and empathizing with their struggles. If you need to talk to someone about your feelings, big or small, I promise there is someone out there who will listen. And I can promise this because one of those is me. Try not to be afraid to ask for help. It takes courage, but it's worth it.

And finally to my dad. You may not be here in person any more, Dad, but you are always with me. It won't be obvious to most people, but this book was inspired by you. You are the hope, the thoughtfulness, the kindness, and the courage in this story. You are Matty's dad, you are Cliff the dog. You are who I strive to be. I know how proud you would be of me right now. I miss you and I love you, Dad. Always. Thank you.

RESOURCES

If you suspect that you or someone you know might have depression or anxiety, consider reaching out to a person you can trust. Or, please contact one of the following organizations for support and further advice.

ANXIETY UK   03444 775 774

MIND   0300 123 3393

NHS   nhs.uk/service-search/mental-health

THE SAMARITANS   Call 116 123

SHOUT   Text SHOUT to 85258

YOUNG MINDS UK   youngminds.org.uk

Remember, asking for help is never a sign of weakness.

Everything is changing for 11-year-old Alex and, as
an autistic person, change can be terrifying. With
the first day of high school only a couple of months
away, Alex is sure that having a friend by his side
will help. So, he's devised a plan – impress the kids
at school by winning a trophy at the PAWS Dog
Show with his trusty sidekick, Kevin. This should
be a walk in the park ... right?

'If you don't believe in magic, you will after you've read *Greenwild*. It's phenomenal.' – A. F. Steadman, author of *Skandar and the Unicorn Thief*

'A spellbinding, enchanting read full of wildness and beauty.' – Hannah Gold, author of *The Last Bear*

'A glorious, page-turning adventure . . . Thomson has created a gorgeous, utterly believable world as magical and magnificent as the Amazon rainforest itself. I adored this book!' – Aisling Fowler, author of *Fireborn*

'*Greenwild* is a thrilling adventure that takes seed in your imagination and runs wild!' – M. G. Leonard, author of *Beetle Boy*

'I fell utterly in love with this sharply beautiful, contemporary adventure.' – Cerrie Burnell, author of *Wilder Than Midnight*

'A wonderfully whimsical story with a beautiful world – and lots of mystery and adventure – for readers to immerse themselves in.' – Aisha Bushby, author of *A Pocketful of Stars*